4.8/5pts

D0559499

# Elsa, Star of the Shelter!

## Jacqueline Wilson

*Illustrated by Nick Sharratt*

Albert Whitman & Company,
Morton Grove, Illinois

*Jacqueline Wilson has written forty books for children. She won the Children's Book Award in 1993 and has been short-listed for the Carnegie Medal three times. She is married and has one daughter, Emma. Jacqueline lives in a small house in Surrey, England, which only just contains her vast collection of ten thousand books!*

Library of Congress Cataloging-in-Publication Data

Wilson, Jacqueline.
   Elsa, star of the shelter! / written by Jacqueline Wilson;
illustrated by Nick Sharratt.
     p.  cm.
   Summary: Noisy, brash, and a troublemaker, ten-year-old Elsa uses her loud
voice to warn of a fire at the homeless shelter where she lives with her family.
   ISBN 0-8075-1981-2
   [1. Homeless persons—Fiction. 2. Family life—Fiction.]
I. Sharratt, Nick, ill. II. Title.
PZ7.W6957E1  1996                                95-3617
[Fic]—dc20                                      CIP
                                                 AC

This work was originally published as *The Bed and Breakfast Star* in 1994 by Doubleday, a division of Transworld Publishers Ltd., London.

Text copyright © 1994 by Jacqueline Wilson.
Illustrations copyright © 1994 by Nick Sharratt.

Published in 1996 by Albert Whitman & Company,
6340 Oakton Street, Morton Grove, Illinois 60053.
Published simultaneously in Canada by
General Publishing, Limited, Toronto.
Printed in the United States of America.
10  9  8  7  6  5  4  3  2  1

# Table of Contents

*For Frances Stokes*
      *(Froggy to her friends)*

# *Chapter 1*

I'm Elsa and I live in England. Not in a house. Not in an apartment.

I live in a bed-and-breakfast hotel. But I'm not on vacation. This is a shelter hotel. We live here because we haven't got anywhere else to go. We get a bed, we get a breakfast—and that's it!

The kids at school yell "Bed and Breakfast" at me. Anyone would think I had a blanket for a blouse, cornflake curls, two fried-egg eyes, and a streaky-bacon smile.

I don't look a bit like that. Well, I hope I don't! I'm Elsa.

Do you like my name? I hope you do like it or Elsa'll get upset. Do you get the joke? I made it up myself. I'm always cracking jokes. People don't often laugh though.

I bet you don't know anyone else called Elsa. There was just this lion called Elsa, ages ago. There was a book written about her, and they made a film. They sometimes show it on the television so maybe you've seen it. My mum named me after Elsa the lion. I was a very tiny baby, smaller than all the others in the hospital, but I was born with lots of hair. Really. Most babies are almost bald but I had this long tufty hair and Mum used to brush it so that it stood out all around my head like a lion's mane. I didn't just look like a lion, I sounded like one too. I might have had very tiny little lungs but I had the loudest voice. I bawled day and night and wore all the nurses out, let alone my mum. She says she should have left me yelling in my hospital bed and slipped away without me. She was joking. Mum's jokes aren't always funny though—not like mine.

That was my very first BED.

It's not very comfy-looking, is it? No wonder I bawled.

Here's my second BED.

I used to pretend I was a real lion in a cage. I really roared.

We've still got my old duck crib. We've lost lots of our other things but we've always carted that around with us. I used to turn it into a play-house

or a car

and once it was even
my castle.

But then my sister Pippa was born and I lost a house and a car and a castle and she gained a bed. I gave it a good spring-cleaning for her and tried to make it as pretty as possible, but I don't think she really appreciated it.

Pippa did a lot more sleeping and a lot less yelling than me. She's not a baby now. She's nearly five. Half my age. She's more than half my size though. She's not a small kid like me. She'll catch up with me soon if I don't watch out.

I've also got a brother, Hank. Hank the Hunk. He had the duck crib too.

He only fit in it for five minutes. I'm tiny and Pippa is tall but Hank is enormous. He's not just long, he's very wide too. He's still not much more than a baby but if you pick him up you practically need a crane and if you put him on your lap you get severely squashed. If you stand in his way when he comes crawling by, then you're likely to get steam-rollered.

Pippa and Hank aren't my real sister and brother. They're halves. That sounds silly, doesn't it. As if they should look like this.

We've all got the same mum. Our mum. But I've got a different dad.

My dad never really lived with Mum and me. He did come and see me sometimes, when I was little. He took me to the zoo to see the real lions.

I can remember it vividly though Mum says I was only about two then. I liked seeing those lions. My dad held me up to see them. They roared at me, and I roared back. I think I maybe went on roaring a bit too long and loud. My dad didn't come back after that.

Mum said we didn't care. We were better off without him. Just Mum and me. That was fine. But then Mum met Mack. Mack the Smack. That's not a joke. He really does smack. Especially me.

You're not supposed to smack children. In lots of countries smacking is against the law and if you hit a child you get sent to prison. I wish I lived in one of those countries. Mack smacks a lot. He doesn't smack Pippa very hard, he just gives her little taps. And he doesn't smack Hank because even Mack doesn't hit babies. But he really whacks me. Well, he doesn't always smack. But he lifts his hand as if he's going to. Or he hisses out of the side of his mouth: "Are you asking for a good smacking, Elsa?"

What sort of question is that, eh? As if I'd prance up to him and say, "Hey, Uncle Mack, can I have a socking big smack, please?"

Mum sometimes sticks up for me. But sometimes she says I'm asking for it too. She says I give Mack a lot of cheek.* I don't. I just try out a few jokes on him, that's all. And he doesn't ever get them. Because he's thick. Thick thick thick as a brick.

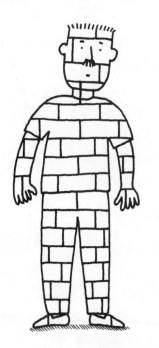

I don't know why my mum had to marry him. And guess who got to be the bridesmaid at their wedding! Mum wanted me to wear a long frilly bridesmaid's dress but it looked ever so silly on me. My hair still sticks out all over the place like a lion's mane and my legs are so skinny my socks always wrinkle and somehow they always get dirty marks all over them and my shoes get all scuffed at the toes right the minute I bring them home from the shop. The bridesmaids' dresses in the shop were

*cheek, cheeky That means I don't show Mack any respect. (Why should I?) I say cheeky; in America, you might say I give Mack a lot of lip or I smart-mouth him.

all pale pink and pale blue and pale peach and pale lilac. Mum sighed and said I'd get my dress dirty before she'd had time to get up and down the aisle.

So we forgot about the dress and instead Mum had me wear this little black velvet jacket and tartan kilt because Mack is Scottish. I even had a sprig of lucky Scottish heather pinned to my jacket. I felt like I needed a bit of luck.

Mack moved in with Mum after the wedding. After I grew out of the duck crib I used to have the big bed with Mum and that was fun because there was always someone to chat with and cuddle.

That was my third BED.

But then Mack got to share the big bed with Mum and I had a little camp bed in the living room. Bed Number Four. And at first I kept falling out of it every time I turned over. But I didn't mind that camp bed. I played camping.

But it was really too cramped to play camp. We only had a little apartment and Mack took up so much *space*.

There certainly wasn't going to be room for a new baby too. (That was Pippa. She wasn't born then. She was just a pipsqueak in Mum's tummy.) Mum had our name down for a bigger apartment but the waiting list was so long it looked like we'd be waiting forever.

Then one of Mack's mates* up in Scotland offered him a new job up there so he went back up to Scotland and we had to go too. We stayed with Mack's mum. I was scared. I thought she might be like Mack.

But she wasn't big, she was little. She didn't smack, but she was really strict all the same. I wasn't allowed to do anything in her house. I couldn't even play properly. She wouldn't let me get all my toys out at once. She said I had to play with them one at a time.

So I started playing with some of her stuff. She had some lovely things—ornaments and photo albums and musical boxes. I didn't break anything at all but she still got mad.

---

*mates Friends. (I'm amazed Mack's got any!) I say mate; you say buddy.

"You're not allowed to go raking through my things! Away and watch the telly* like a good wee bairn."*

That's all you were supposed to do in her house. Watch the telly. We watched it all the time.

My Scottish sort-of Gran wasn't so bad though. She did pass the sweets* round while we were watching her telly. She called them sweeties.

"Are you wanting a sweetie, hen?" she'd say to me.

*telly* TV
*bairn* Scottish for kid. Me!
*sweets* candy
Now translate: All bairns like watching telly and eating sweets.

And I'd go cluck-cluck-cluck and flap my arms and she'd laugh and say I could be awfully funny when I wanted. On Sundays we had special sweeties, a homemade fudge she called tablet. Oh, that tablet. Yum yum YUM.

I could eat tablet all day long. I didn't eat much else at my sort-of Gran's. She said I was a poor wee bairn who needed fattening up but she kept giving me plates of mince and tatties. I don't like minced beef because it looks as if someone has already chewed it, and I don't like mashed potatoes because I'm always scared there's going to be a lump. So I didn't eat much and she got cross with me and Mum got cross with me and Mack got cross with me.

The worse bit about living there was the bed. Bed Number Five. Only it wasn't my bed, it was my sort-of Gran's. I had to share it with her. There wasn't room in her bedroom for my camp bed, you see, and she said she didn't want it cluttering up her living room. She liked it when I stopped cluttering up the place too. She was always wanting to whisk me away to bed early. I was generally still awake when she came in. I used to peek when she took her corset off.

She wasn't so little when that corset was off. She took up a lot of the bed once she was in it. Sometimes I'd end up clutching the edge, hanging on for dear life. And another thing. She snored.

We were meant to be looking for our own place in Scotland but we never found one. Then my sister Pippa got born and Mack had a fight with his pal and lost his job. Mum got ever so worried. She didn't get along very well with my sort-of Gran and it got worse after Pippa was born.

So we moved back down South and said we were homeless. Mum got even more worried. She thought we'd be put in a bed-and-breakfast hotel. She said she'd never live it down. (Little did she know. You don't have to live it down. You can live it *up*.)

But we didn't get put in a shelter hotel then. We were offered this apartment in a tough area. It was dirty and disgusting, but Mack said he'd fix it up so it would look like a palace. So we moved in. It was a pretty weirdo palace, if you ask me. There was green mold on the walls and creepy-crawlies in the kitchen. Mack tried slapping a bit of paint about but it didn't make much difference. Mum got ever so depressed and Mack got cross. Pippa kept getting coughs and colds and snuffling, because it was so damp.

I was OK though. My camp bed collapsed once and for all, so I got to have a new bed.

Bed Number Six. It had springs and it made the most wonderful trampoline.

I had a lot of fun in that apartment building.
I didn't want to leave.

But Mack got his
new job and started
to make a lot of
money and he said
he'd buy Mum her
own house and Mum
was over the moon.

Yippee!

I thought it was great once we'd moved into the new house. I liked that house ever so much. It wasn't damp. It was warm and cozy and when Pippa and I got up we could run about in our pajamas without getting a bit cold. Pippa stopped being a boring old baby and started to play the right way. She shared my new bed now and I didn't really mind that much because she liked my stories and she actually laughed at my jokes. We kept getting the giggles late at night

when we were supposed to be asleep, but Mum didn't often get cross and Mack didn't even smack anymore. Hank the Hunk got born and he was happy too.

But we didn't live happily ever after.

Mack's job ended. He got another but it didn't pay nearly so well. And then he lost that one. And he couldn't get another. Mum worked in a supermarket while Mack looked after Pippa and Hank. (*I* can look after myself.)

But Mum's money wouldn't pay all the bills. It wouldn't pay for the lovely new house. So some people came and took nearly all our things away. We had to leave our new house. I cried. So did Pippa and Hank. Mum cried too. Mack didn't cry, but he looked as if he might.

We thought we'd have to go back to the moldy apartment. But they'd put another family in there. There wasn't any room for us.

So guess where we ended up. In a bed-and-breakfast hotel.

# Chapter 2

We went to stay at the Royal Hotel. The Royal sounds very grand, doesn't it? And when we were down one end of the street and got our first glimpse of the Royal right at the other end, I thought it looked very grand too. I started to get excited. I'd never stayed in a great big fancy

hotel before. Maybe we'd all have our own rooms with cable telly and people would make our beds and serve us our breakfasts from silver trays. As if we were Royalty staying in the Royal.

But the Royal started to look a bit shabby the nearer we got. We saw it needed painting. We saw one of the windows was broken and patched with cardboard. We saw the big gilt lettering was all wobbly and some of it was missing. We were going to be staying in the oyal H t l.

"O Yal Htl," I said. It sounded funny. "O Yal Htl," I repeated. I thought of a song we sang at school about an old man river who just went rolling along. "O Yal Htl," I sang to the same tune.

"Will you just shut it, Elsa?" said Mack the Smack.

"I can't shut, I'm not a door," I said. "Hey, when is a door not a door? When it's ajar!"

No one laughed. Mum looked as if she was about to cry. She was staring up at the Royal, shaking her head.

"No," she said. "No, no, no." She started off quietly enough, but her voice got louder and louder. *"No, no, no!"*

"Come on, it's maybe not that bad," said Mack, putting his arm round her.

Mum was carrying Hank. He got a bit squashed and started squawking. Pippa's mouth quivered and she tried to clutch at Mum too.

"I don't like this place, Mum," she said. "We don't have to go and live here, do we?"

"No, we don't, kids. We're not living in a dump like this," said Mum. She kicked the litter in the driveway. An old carton of Chinese take-away* leaked orange liquid all over her suede shoes.

"For heaven's sake," Mum wept. "Look at all this muck. There'll be rats. And if it's like this outside, what's it going to be like inside? Cockroaches. Fleas. I'm not taking my kids into a lousy dump like this."

"So where are you going to take them?" said Mack. "Come on, answer me. Where?"

Hank cried harder. Pippa sniffed and stuck her thumb in her mouth. I fiddled with my hair. Mum pressed her lips tight together, as if she was rubbing in her lipstick. Only she wasn't wearing any makeup at all. Her face was as white as ice cream. When I tried to take her hand, her fingers were cold as ice too.

She shook her head. She didn't know how to

*take-away* Ready-cooked hot food. I buy take-away food, you buy take-out food.

answer Mack. She didn't have any other place to take us.

"I'm sorry," said Mack. "I've failed you, haven't I?" He suddenly didn't seem so big anymore. It was if he were shrinking inside his clothes.

"Oh don't be silly," said Mum wearily. She joggled Hank and wiped Pippa's nose and tried to pat my hair into place. We all wriggled and protested. "It's not your fault, Mack."

"Well, whose fault is it then?" Mack mumbled. "I've let you down. I can't get work, I can't even provide a proper home for you and the kids."

"It's not your fault. It's not anybody's fault. It's just . . . circumstances," said Mum.

I saw a horrible snooty old gent, Sir Come-Stances, pointing his fat finger in our direction while all his servants snatched our house and our furniture and our television and our toys. I was so busy thinking about him that I hardly noticed Mum marching off into the entrance of the Royal, Hank on one hip, Pippa hanging on her arm. Mack shuffled after her, carrying all our stuff. He turned around when he got to the revolving door.

"Elsa!" he called irritably. "Don't just stand there looking like a dope. Come on!"

"It takes one to know one, Mack!"

"*Elsa!* Are you asking for a good smacking?"

I decided it was time to hurry after him. I squashed into the doorway and pushed hard. It bumped against Mack's leg and he yelled and stumbled out the other side, cursing. I stayed revolving around the door by myself. I felt as if I wanted to go on spinning and spinning. Maybe if I twirled really fast like a top then there would be this humming sound and everything would blur and I'd shoot out into somewhere else entirely, a warm bright world where everyone liked me and laughed at my jokes.

I stepped into the grubby lobby of the Royal Hotel instead. There was a dark carpet on the floor, red with lots of stains. The thick wallpaper was red too, with a crusty pattern like dried blood. The ceiling was studded with white plastic tiles but several were missing. I wondered if anyone had gone away wearing one as a hat without noticing.

There was a big counter with a bell. We could see through a glass door behind the counter into an office. A woman was sitting in there, eating sweets out of a paper bag and reading a big fat book. She didn't seem to notice us, even though Hank was crying and Mack was creating a commotion hauling all our cases and plastic bags around the revolving doors and into the hallway.

Mum touched the bell on the counter. It gave a brisk trill. The woman popped another peardrop in her mouth and turned a page of her novel. Mum cleared her throat loudly and pinged on the bell. I hit it too. Then Pippa. The woman turned her back on us with one swivel of her chair.

"Oi! You in there!" Mack bellowed, thumping his big fist on the counter.

The woman put down her book with a sigh, marking her place with a sweet wrapper. She stretched out her arm and opened the glass door a fraction.

"There's no need to take that tone. Manners don't cost a penny," she said in a pained voice.

"Well, we did ring the bell," said Mum. "You must have heard it."

"Yes, but it's nothing to do with me. I'm only telephone. That bell's for management."

"But there doesn't seem to *be* any management," said Mum. "This is ridiculous."

"If you want to make a complaint you must put it in writing and give it to the Manager."

"Where is this Manager then?" asked Mack.

"I've no idea. I told you, it's nothing to do with me. I'm only telephone." She closed her glass door and stuck her nose back in her book.

"I don't believe this," said Mum. "It's a total nightmare."

I shut my eyes tight, hoping like mad that it really was a nightmare. I badly wanted to be back in bouncy bed number six in the lovely new house. I put my hands over my ears to blot out Hank's bawling and tried hard to dream myself back into that bed. I felt I was very nearly there ... but then Mack's big hand shook my shoulder.

"What are you playing at, Elsa? Stop screwing up your face like that, you look like you're having a fit or something," said Mack.

I glared and shook my shoulder free. I shuffled away from him, scuffing my trainers* on the worn carpet. I saw a door at the end of the hallway. It had a nameplate.

I pushed the door open and peeked round. There was a little man in a brown suit sitting at a desk. A big lady in a fluffy pink sweater was sitting at the desk too. She was perched on the man's lap and they were *kissing*. When they saw me the lady leapt up, going pink in the face to match her sweater. The little man seemed to be catching his breath. No wonder. The lady was *very* big, especially in certain places.

*trainers* Training shoes. Mine are from a discount store. I wish I had a super cool brand-name pair. I say trainers; you say sneakers or gym shoes.

"Excuse me," I said politely. After all, I'd just been told that manners don't cost a penny.

"Come on now, out of here," said the big lady shooing at me as if I was a stray cat. "And don't hang around the reception area either. I'm sick and tired of you kids turning this hotel into a playground. You go up to your room, do you hear me?"

"That's right. Go to your room, little girly," said the man in the brown suit, trying to brush all the little pink hairs away.

"But I haven't *got* a room," I said. "We've only just come here and we don't know where to go."

"Well, why didn't you say so?" said the fluffy

pink lady, and she flounced out of the room, beckoning me with one of her long pink fingernails.

Hank was still howling out in the hall. Pippa was whispering and Mum was muttering and Mack was pacing the carpet like a caged animal, looking as if he was ready to bite someone.

"*So* sorry to have kept you waiting," said the

big lady, and she hurried around the corner of the counter and smiled a big lipsticky smile. "On behalf of the management, I'd like to welcome you to the Royal Hotel. I hope your stay with us will be a pleasant one."

"Well, we're hardly here on holiday," said

Mum, wrestling with Hank. She sat him down on the counter to give her arms a rest. Hank perked up a little. He spotted what looked like a very very big pink bunny rabbit and started crawling rapidly toward it, drooling joyfully.

"Please try to keep your children under control!" said the big lady, swatting nervously at the advancing baby. "I'll have to get some information from you."

This took forever. Hank howled mournfully, deprived of his cuddle with the giant pink bunny. Mum sighed. Mack tutted and strutted, working himself up into a temper. Pippa started hopping about and holding herself. There was going to be a puddle on the carpet if we didn't watch out.

"Mum, Pippa has to go to the toilet," I hissed.

"Shut *up*, Elsa," said Pippa, squirming.

Mum cast an experienced eye at Pippa.

"You'd better take her, Elsa," she said.

The big lady paused and pointed the way down the hall and around the corner. I took Pippa's arm and hurried her along. We passed the Manager's office. His door was ajar. Like my joke.

We had a quick peek at him. He was still sitting at his desk. He'd kicked his shoes off and put his feet up. One of his socks had a hole.

His toe stuck through and looked so silly that

Pippa and I got the giggles. The Manager heard and looked cross and we scooted quickly down the corridor. We had to dash anyway because it was getting a bit risky for Pippa to be laughing in her current circumstances.

Things got riskier still because we seemed to take a wrong turn and blundered around, unable to find the toilets. We came across a gang of boys as we rounded a corner. They were busy writing something on the wall with black felt-tip pen.

"Don't ask them, they'll laugh at us," said Pippa urgently.

They laughed at us anyway, making rude comments as we rushed past. You know the sort of things boys shout out.

"They are *rude*," said Pippa.

They were ruder than Pippa realized. She

can't read yet. *I* read what they were writing on the wall.

We hurried on, turned another corner, and suddenly I saw one of those funny little lady outlines stuck up on the door.

I don't know why they design the lady in that weird sticky-out dress. And she hasn't got any arms, poor thing, so she'd have a hard time using the loo* herself, especially when it came to pulling the chain.

I was still busy thinking about this little lady as Pippa charged inside. I heard the door bang shut.

"Did you make it in time, Pippa?" I called.

"Shut *up*," Pippa called back.

It sounded as if her teeth were gritted. I stepped inside to find out why. There was someone else there. A girl about my own age was sitting on the windowsill with her feet propped on

---

*loo This is a slang name for toilet. It's a polite word. (I know lots of rude words for the toilet and I bet you do too!) Some English loos have their water tanks very high up, so you have to pull a chain to flush them. I say loo, you say john. Do the outline ladies on loos in the United States have arms on them?

the edge of the sink. She was reading a book. Well, she had her eyes on the page, but you could tell we were disturbing her.

"Hello," I said.

She nodded at me, looking a bit nervous.

"I'm Elsa. And that's my sister Pippa sitting on the toilet."

"Don't keep *telling* everyone!" Pippa shouted from inside.

"Sisters!" I said, raising my eyebrows.

"Brothers are worse," said the girl. "I've got three."

"I've got one too. He's only a baby but he's still awful. I have to look after him sometimes."

"I have to look after my brothers all of the time. Only I get fed up because they keep pestering me. So sometimes I slip in here for a little peace."

"Good idea. So what's your name, then?"

"Naomi."

"Hi, Naomi, I'm Elsa."

"Yes, you said."

"How long have you been here?"

"Sitting in the sink?"

"No! In this place. The hotel."

"About six months."

"You haven't! Gosh."

I was too busy thinking to talk any more. I'd thought we'd stay in the hotel a week or two at the most. As if we really were on holiday. I hadn't realized we might be stuck here for months and months.

Pippa pulled the chain and came out of the toilet. Naomi swung her skinny legs out of the way so that Pippa could wash her hands. There weren't any towels so I let Pippa wipe her hands on my T-shirt. Naomi settled her feet back again.

I looked at her. I looked at the tap.

"I could give your feet a little paddle," I said.

"Don't," said Naomi.

I thought about it.

"OK."

I smiled at her. She smiled back. Things were looking up. I'd only just got here and I'd already made a friend.

I took Pippa's damp hand and we set off back down the corridor.

"I like that girl," said Pippa.

"That's my friend. Naomi."

"She can be my friend too. I like her hair. All the little braids. Will you do my hair like that, Elsa?"

"It looks a bit too fiddly. Come on, quick." We were going past the boys again. They said some more rude things. Really awful things.

"You think you're so clever, but you can't even

spell," I said, snatching the felt-tip. I crossed out the worst word and wrote it correctly.

That showed them. They muttered the word several times. Pippa and I skipped on down the corridor and eventually found our way back to the lobby.

"There you are! I was beginning to think you'd gotten lost," said Mum.

The big lady was handing a key to Mack.

"One room for all five of us?" said Mack.

"It's a family room, with full facilities."

Mack stared at the number tag.

"Room six-oh-eight?"

"That's right."

"That doesn't mean we're up on the sixth floor, does it?"

"You got it."

"But we've got little kids. You can't shove us right up at the top—it's stupid."

"It's the only room available at the moment. Sorry," said the big lady, fluffing up her sweater.

"There is a lift?"* said Mum.

"Oh yes, there's a lift," said the big lady. "Only the kids have been messing around and it's not

---

*lift A little room that goes up and down between floors and makes your tummy flip over. I say lift, you say elevator.

working at the moment. We're getting it fixed tomorrow. Meanwhile the stairs are over there."

It took us a long while and several journeys to get us and all our stuff up those stairs.

But at long last we were all crowded into room 608. Our new home.

# Chapter 3

I thought a family room would have room for a family. Something like this:

Only room 608 wasn't quite how I'd imagined. It was a bit cramped to say the least. And by the time we'd squeezed inside with all our stuff, we couldn't even breathe without bumping into each other.

"Home sweet home," said Mum, and she burst into tears.

"Don't start on the waterworks," said Mack. "Come on, hen, it's not as bad as all that."

"It's worse," said Mum, trying to swallow her sobs. It sounded as if she was clucking. Like a hen. Mack calls her that when he's trying to be nice. And he sometimes calls Pippa "ma wee chook" which is probably Scottish for chick. Hank is too big to be a chick. He's more like a turkey. I don't get called anything. I am not part of Mack's personal farmyard.

I stepped over all our stuff and climbed across a bed or two and made it to the window. It was probably a good thing it had bars, especially with Hank starting to pull himself up. He'd be able to climb soon and he's got so little sense he'd go right to the window first thing. But I didn't like the bars all the same. It felt as if we were all in a cage.

It wasn't just us and our family. We could hear the people in room 607 having an argument. And the people in room 609 had their television on so loudly it made our room buzz with the conversation. The people underneath us in room 508 were playing heavy-metal music and the floor bumped up and down with the beat. At least the sixth floor was the top floor, so there was no one up above us making a racket.

"It's bedlam," said Mum.

Bedlam is some old prison place where they used to put people who had mental illness, but it made me think of beds. I flopped down onto one of the single beds. It gave a creak and a groan.

I didn't bounce a bit on this bed. I just jumped to a halt. Bed Number Seven was a disappointment.

I tried another single bed, just in case that was better. It was worse. The mattress sagged right down through the bedsprings. I set them all jangling as I jumped on and on.

"Elsa! Will you quit that!" Mack yelled.

"I was just trying out my bed, that's all. Figuring out where we're all going to sleep."

I decided to crack a bed joke to cheer us up. "Hey, where do apes sleep?"

"Give it a rest, Elsa, eh?" Mum sniffed.

"No, listen, it's good this one, really. Where do apes sleep? Can't you guess? Apes sleep in apricots." I waited. They didn't even titter. "*Apricots*," I said clearly, in case they hadn't got it the first time around.

"Sh! Keep your voice down. Everyone can hear what you're saying," said Mum.

"Then why isn't everybody laughing?" I said. "Look, don't you get it? Apes sleep in . . ."

"That's *enough!*" Mack thundered. "Button that lip."

Honestly!

Then I had to unbutton, because I'd just thought of something.

"What about Hank? There isn't a bed for him," I said.

We all looked round the room, as if a bed might suddenly appear out of nowhere.

"This will be Hank's little bedroom in here," said Pippa, opening a cupboard door that stuck right out into the room, taking up even more of the space. It wasn't another bedroom. It was the shower and the loo and the washbasin, all cramped in together.

"We're going to be able to save time, you know. I reckon you could sit on the loo and clean your teeth and stick your feet in the shower all at the same time," I said. "Let's try it."

"Look, come out of there, Elsa, and stop mucking about," said Mum. "This is ridiculous. Where is Hank going to sleep?"

"I'll go downstairs and tell them we need another bed," said Mack.

"Yes, but where are we going to put it?" said Mum. "There's no room to move as it is."

"Maybe we'll have to take turns moving," I said. "You and Mack could stand in the shower while Pippa and Hank and I play for a bit, and then you could yell 'All change!' and we'll cram into the shower and you two could walk around and around the beds for a bit of exercise."

I thought it an extremely sensible idea but they didn't think so.

"You'll be the one standing in the shower if you don't watch it," said Mack. "And the cold water will be on too." He laughed. That's his idea of a joke.

He went all the way downstairs to tackle the big lady about another bed. Mum sat on the edge of the double bed, staring into space. Her eyes were watery again. She didn't notice when Hank got into her handbag and started licking her lipstick as if it was a popsicle. I grabbed him and hauled him into the tiny shower space to mop him up a bit. The hot water in the basin was only lukewarm. I tried the shower to see if that water was hot. I couldn't figure out how to switch it on. Pippa squeezed in to give me a hand. I suddenly found the right knob to turn. I turned it a bit too far actually.

Mack's joke came true. It wasn't very funny. But at least we all got clean. Our clothes had a quick wash too. I dried us off as best I could. I thought Mum might get mad but she didn't say a word. She just went on staring, as if she was looking right through the wall into room 607. They were still having their argument. It was getting louder. They were starting to use a lot of rude words.

"Uh-oh!" said Pippa, giggling.

Mack came storming back and he was mumbling a lot of rude words too. The hotel management didn't supply beds for children under two. "Hank will have to go back to his crib," he said and he started putting the old duck crib together again.

"But it's falling to bits now. And Hank's so big and bouncy. He kept thumping and jumping last time he was in it. He'll smash it up in seconds," I said.

"And that's not Hank's crib anymore. It's my Baby Pillow's bed," said Pippa indignantly.

"Baby Pillow will have to sleep with you, ma wee chook," said Mack.

"But he won't like that. Baby Pillow will cry and kick me," said Pippa.

"Well, you'll just have to cry and kick him

back," said Mack, reaching out and giving her a little poke in the tummy. He noticed her T-shirt was a little damp.

"Here, how come you're soaking wet?" said Mack, frowning.

I held my breath. If Pippa told on me I'd really be in for it. And five it and six it too.

But Pippa was a pal. She just mumbled something about splashing herself, so Mack grunted and went on setting up the duck crib for Hank. I gratefully helped Pippa find Baby Pillow and all his things from one of the black plastic rubbish bags we'd carted from our old house.

My sister Pippa is funny. Mack was always buying her dolls when he was working and we were rich. All the different Barbies, My Little Ponies, those big special dolls that walk and talk and wet, but the only doll Pippa's ever loved is Baby Pillow. Baby Pillow got born when Mum had Hank. Pippa started carting this old pillow round with her, talking to it and rocking it as if it were a baby. He's rather a backward baby if he's as old as Hank, because

he hasn't started crawling yet. If I'm feeling in a very good mood I help Pippa feed Baby Pillow with one of Hank's old bottles and we change his old nappy* and bundle him up into an old nightie and then we tuck him into the duck crib and tell him to go to sleep. I generally make him cry quite a bit first and Pippa has to keep rocking him and telling him stories.

"We won't be able to play our game if Hank's got to go in the duck crib," Pippa grumbled.

But when Mack had got the crib standing in the last available spot of space and we tried stuffing Hank into his old baby bed, Hank himself decided this just wasn't on. He howled indignantly and started rocking the bars and cocking his leg up, trying to escape.

*nappy, nappies Pads you put on babies to stop them from wetting their clothes—or worse! I say nappy, you say diaper.

"He'll be out in no time," said Mack. "So what are we going to do, eh?"

He looked over at Mum. She was still staring into space. She was acting as if she couldn't hear Mack or even Hank's bawling.

"Mum?" said Pippa, and she clutched Baby Pillow anxiously.

"Hey, Mum," I said, and I went and shook her shoulder. She wasn't crying anymore. This was worse. She didn't even notice me.

"Here," said Mack, grabbing Hank, hauling him out of the crib and dumping him into Mum's lap.

For a moment Mum kept her arms limply by her sides, her face still blank. Hank howled harder, hurt that he was getting ignored. He raised his arms, wanting a hug. He stretched higher, lost his balance, and nearly toppled right off Mum's lap and onto the floor. But just in time Mum's hands grabbed him and pulled him close against her chest.

"Don't cry. I've got you," said Mum sighing. She blinked, back to herself.

"Where's the wee boy going to sleep, then?" Mack asked again.

Mum shrugged.

"He'll have to sleep with one of his sisters,

won't he," she said.

"Not me!" I said quickly.

"Not me either," said Pippa. "He wets right out of his nappies."

Hank went on crying.

"He's hungry," said Mum. "We could all do with a drink and a bite to eat. I'm going to go and find the kitchen. Here Hank, go to Daddy. And you girls, you get all our stuff unpacked from those bags, okay?"

Yes, everything was all right again. Mum rolled up her sleeves and got the cardboard box with our kettle and our pots and pans and some cans of food and went off to find the kitchen. Mack romped on the bed with Hank, and he stopped crying and started chuckling. Pippa said Baby Pillow was still crying though, and she insisted she had to get him into the duck crib and put him to sleep.

So I got stuck doing most of the unpacking. There were two bags full of Pippa's clothes and Hank's baby stuff. There was an old suitcase filled with Mum and Mack's clothes and Mum's hair dryer and her makeup and her precious china lady with the lacy skirt. And there was my carrier bag. I don't have that many clothes because I always get them mucked up anyway. I've got T-shirts and shorts for the summer, and sweaters and jeans for the winter, and some knickers* and socks and stuff. I've got a Minnie Mouse hairbrush though it doesn't ever get all the tangles out of my mane of hair. I've got a green marble that I used to pretend was magic. I've got my box of felt-tip pens. Most of the colors have run out and Pippa mucked up some of the points when she was little, but I don't feel like throwing them away yet. Sometimes I color a ghost picture, pretending the colors in my head. Then there are my joke books. They are a bit torn and tattered because I thumb through them so often.

I hoped Mum would be ever so pleased with me getting all our stuff sorted out and the room all neat and tidy but she came back so flaming mad she hardly noticed.

"This is ridiculous," she said, dumping the cardboard box so violently that all the pots and pans played a tune. "I had to queue up* for ages just to get into this crummy little kitchen, and

*knickers This is getting personal! Knickers means underwear. I say underwear, you say underpants. We say underpants too, but only for the shorts that men wear.
*queue up Stand and wait your turn, not always patiently! I say queue up, you say stand in line. A queue is the line you wait in.

then when some of these other women were finished and I got my chance, I realized that it was all a waste of time anyway. You should see the state of that stove! It's filthy. I'd have to scrub at it for a week before I'd set my saucepans on it. Even the floor's so slimy with grease I nearly slipped and fell. What are we going to do, Mack?"

"You're asking Big Mack, right?" said Mack, throwing Hank up in the air so he shrieked with delight. "Big Mack says let's go and eat Big Macs at McDonald's."

Pippa and I shrieked with delight too. Mum didn't look so thrilled.

"And what are we going to live on for the rest of the week, eh?" she said. "We can't eat out all the time, Mack."

"Come on now, hen, give it a rest. You just now said we can't eat in. So we'll eat out today. Tomorrow will just have to take care of itself."

"The sun will come out tooomorrow . . ." I sang. I maybe don't have a very sweet voice but it is strong.

"Elsa! Keep your voice down!" Mum hissed.

Mack made a silly face and covered up his ears, pretending to be deafened.

We sang the Tomorrow song at school. It comes from a musical about a little orphan girl called Annie. Occasionally I think I'd rather like to be Little Orphan Elsa.

Still, I cheered up considerably because McDonald's is one of my all-time favorite places. Mum changed Hank and we all got ready to go out. It was odd using the little loo in the bedroom. Pippa didn't like it with everybody listening so I went down the hall with her to find another ladies' toilet. We found one, but it was disgusting. I knew if Mum found it, she'd get flaming mad again. Pippa didn't want to use it, but by now she was hopping about agitatedly, so I ended up trailing her down six flights of stairs and along the main hall to the toilet where we'd met Naomi. I hoped she might still be there, but she'd gone. The boys weren't hanging around anymore either. The rude words were still on the wall though.

We'd worked up quite an appetite by the time we'd trudged up the stairs to put on our sweaters and then down all over again with Mum and Mack and Hank.

It was a long, long walk into town to find the McDonald's. Pippa started to lag behind and Mum kept twisting her ankle in her high heels. I started to get pretty tired too, and my toes rubbed up against the edge of my trainers because they're getting too small for me. Mum moaned about being stuck in a dump of a hotel at the edge of nowhere and said she couldn't walk another step. Mack stopped at a phone box and said he'd call a cab, and Mum said he was crazy and it was no wonder we'd all ended up in a shelter.

It was starting to sound like a very big fight. I was getting scared that we'd maybe end up with no tea* at all. But then we got to a bus stop and a bus came along and we all climbed on and we were in town in no time. At McDonald's.

Mack had his Big Mac. Mum had chicken nuggets. I chose a cheeseburger and Pippa did too because she always copies me. Hank nibbled his own chips* and experienced his very first strawberry milkshake.

It was great. We didn't have a big fight.

---

*tea* Grand old ladies in England have afternoon tea—that's dainty sandwiches and special cake and cups of tea. I'm not a grand old lady — I'm an ordinary little kid and our tea is our evening meal, eaten any old time between five and eight in the evening. My favorite tea is burgers and French fries and a milkshake. I say tea, you say supper.
*chips* Fried sliced potatoes. Yummy yummy. I say chips, you say French fries.

We didn't even have a little one. We sat in the warm restaurant, feeling full, and Mack pulled Pippa onto his lap and Mum put her arm around me, and Hank nodded off in his buggy still clutching a handful of chips.

We looked like an ordinary happy family having a meal out. But we didn't go back to an ordinary happy family house. We had to go back to the bed-and-breakfast hotel.

The people in 607 were still arguing. The people in 609 still had their television blaring. The people in 508 were still into heavy-metal music. And we were even more squashed in room 608.

We all went to bed because there wasn't much else to do. Mum and Mack in the double bed. Pippa and Hank at either end of one single bed. Me in the other. Baby Pillow the comfiest of all in the duck crib.

Hank wasn't the only one who wet in the night. Pippa did too, so she had to creep in with me. She went back to sleep right away, but I didn't. I wriggled around uncomfortably, Pippa's hair tickling my nose and her elbow digging into my chest. I stared up into the dark while Mack snored and Hank snuffled and I wished I could rise out of my crowded bed right through the roof and up into the starry sky.

# Chapter 4

We've always had different breakfasts. Mum's never really bothered. She just likes a cup of coffee. She says she can't think about food early in the morning. She cooks for Mack though. He likes great greasy bacon sandwiches and a cup of strong tea with four spoonfuls of sugar. I'd like four spoonfuls of sugar in my tea but Mum won't let me. It's not fair. She does sometimes let me have a sugar sandwich for my breakfast though, if she's in a very good mood. I say *she* needs to eat a sugar sandwich to sweeten herself up.

Pippa likes sugar sandwiches too, because she always copies me. Hank has a runny boiled egg that runs all over him. His face is bright yellow by the time he's finished his breakfast, and he

always insists on clutching his buttered toast until he's squeezed it into a soggy pulp. Sometimes I can see why Mum can't face food herself. Mopping up my baby brother would make anyone lose her appetite.

Mum certainly didn't look like she wanted any breakfast our first morning at the Royal. She'd obviously tossed and turned a lot in the night because her hair was all sticking up at the back. Her eyes looked red and sore. I'd heard her crying in the night.

"How about you taking the kids down to breakfast, Mack?" she said pleadingly. "I don't think I could face it today. I'm feeling ever so queasy."

"Aw, come on, hen. I can't cope with all three of them on my own. I'm not Mary Piddly Poppins."

"You don't have to cope with me," I said indignantly.

"I often wish I didn't," Mack growled.

He's always like that with me. Ready to bite my head off. He's the one who's like a lion, not me.

I wish I could figure out some way of taming him.

"I'll feed Hank for you, Mum, and see that Pippa has a proper breakfast," I promised kindly.

"Your mum's going to have a proper breakfast herself," said Mack. "That's what she needs to make her feel better. A good cooked breakfast. And if we're getting it as part of this lousy bed-and-breakfast deal then we ought to make sure we all eat every last mouthful."

"All right, I'm coming," said Mum, slapping a

bit of makeup on her pale face and fiddling with her hair. She took out her mirror from her handbag and winced. "I look a sight," she wailed.

"You look fine to me," said Mack, giving her powdered cheek a kiss. "And you'll look even better once you've got a fried egg and a few strips of bacon inside you."

"Don't, Mack! You're going to make me throw up," said Mum.

*I'd* throw up if Mack started slobbering at me like that.

We trailed down all the stairs to the ground floor, where this breakfast room was supposed to be. Mack started sniffing, his hairy nostrils all aquiver.

"Can't smell any bacon sizzling," he said.

We soon found out why. There wasn't any bacon for breakfast. There wasn't very much of anything. Just pots of tea and bowls of cornflakes and slices of bread, very white and very square, like the ceiling tiles in the lobby. You just went and served yourself and sat at one of the tables.

"No bacon?" said Mack, and he stormed off to the reception desk.

"Hank needs his egg," said Mum, and she marched off after Mack, Hank balanced on her hip.

Pippa and I sighed and shrugged our shoulders. We straggled off after them.

The big lady was behind the desk. She was wearing a fluffy blue sweater this time. I hoped she'd painted her fingernails blue to match but she hadn't. Still, Mack was certainly turning the air blue, shouting and swearing because there weren't any cooked breakfasts.

"It's your duty to provide a proper breakfast. They said so down at Social Services. I'm going to report you," Mack thundered.

"We don't have any duty whatsoever, sir. If you don't care to stay at the Royal Hotel then why don't you leave?" said the big lady.

RECEPTION

"You know very well we can't leave, because we haven't got anywhere else to go. And it's a disgrace. My kids need a good breakfast and my baby boy needs his protein or he'll get ill," said Mum.

She spoke as if Hank was on the point of starving right this minute, although she was sagging sideways trying to support her great strapping son. He was reaching longingly for this new blue bunny.

The big lady stepped backwards, away from his sticky clasp.

"We're providing extra milk for all the children at the moment. We normally do provide a full cooked breakfast but unfortunately we are temporarily between breakfast chefs, so in these circumstances we can only offer a continental breakfast. Take it—or leave it."

We decided to take it.

"Continental breakfast!" said Mum, as we sat at a table in the corner. "That's coffee in a nice pot and croissants, not this sort of rubbish." She flapped one of the limp slices of bread in the air. "There's no nutrition in this!"

There were little packets of butter and jars of marmalade. And sugar cubes. Lots of sugar cubes.

I got busy crushing and sprinkling. I made myself a splendid sugar sandwich. Pippa tried to make herself one too, but she wasn't much good at crushing the lumps. She tried bashing them hard on the table to make them shatter.

"Pippa! Please stop it, for goodness sake. Whatever are you doing?" said Mum, spooning cornflakes into Hank.

"It's Elsa's fault. Pippa's just copying her," said Mack. "Here, give me that sugar bowl and stop messing around. You'll rot your teeth and just have empty gums by the time you're twelve."

I covered my teeth with my lips and made little gulpy noises to see what it would be like with empty gums. I tried sucking at my sandwich to see if I'd still be able to eat without teeth. I swallowed before the lump in my mouth got soft enough, and choked.

"Elsa! Look, do you have to embarrass us all?" Mum hissed.

"Stop it!" said Mack. "Otherwise you'll get a good smacking, see?"

I saw. I was trying like anything to stop choking. I got up, coughing and spluttering and went over to get myself some more milk. There was a big black lady holding a baby and serving herself. I wondered if she might be Naomi's mum and asked her between coughs.

She said she wasn't, but helpfully banged me on the back. I took a long drink of milk and peered all round the room, hoping to spot Naomi. There were old people and young people and lots of little kids, black people and white people and brown people and yellow people, quiet people and noisy people and absolutely bawling babies. But I couldn't spot Naomi anywhere. Maybe she had her breakfast sitting in the washbasin in the Ladies' Room.

I did spot one of the boys who'd been writing rude words all over the wall. He saw me looking at him and crossed his eyes and stuck out his tongue. I did likewise.

"Elsa!" Mum came and yanked me back to our table. "Don't you dare make faces like that."

I made another face, because I was getting fed up with everyone picking on me when it wasn't my fault. Then I saw a lovely lady with lots of little braids come into the breakfast room. She had two little boys with her, and she was carrying a toddler. And a girl followed on behind, her head in a book.

"NAOMI!" I yelled excitedly, jumping up.

Mack was taking a large gulp of tea at that precise second. Somehow or other the tea sprayed all down his front. He didn't look too happy. I decided to dash over to Naomi pretty fast.

"Hi, Naomi. I've been looking out for you. Is this your mum? Are these your brothers?"

I said hello to them all and they smiled and said hello back.

"Is that your dad over there? That man shouting at you," said Naomi.

"Don't worry," I said. "What are you reading?"

I had a quick look. The cover said *Little Women* and there was a picture of four girls in old-fashioned dresses.

"*Little Women*?" I asked.

"It's a lovely book, one of the classics," said Naomi's mum proudly. "My Naomi's always reading it."

"Boring," I mumbled, peering at the pages.

*"The Cursed Werewolf seized the young maiden and ripped her to pieces with his huge yellow teeth . . ."*

"There's a werewolf in *Little Women?*" I said, astonished.

"Sh!" said Naomi, giving me a nudge. She turned her back so that her mum couldn't see and quickly lifted the dust jacket off *Little Women*. She had a different book underneath: *The Cursed Werewolf Runs Wild.*

"Ah," I said. I decided I liked Naomi even more.

I sat down at their table, even though Mack was bellowing fit to bust for me to come back at once OR ELSE. Naomi's little brothers looked utterly angelic above the table, all big eyes and smiley mouths, but they were conducting a violent kicking match out of sight. One of the kicks landed right on my kneecap. I gave a little scream and both boys looked anxiously at their mum. I didn't tell tales, but I seized hold of several skinny legs and tickled unmercifully. They squirmed and doubled up.

"Boys!" said Naomi's mum. "Stop messing about."

She was trying to feed the baby but he kept fidgeting and turning his head away, not wanting his soggy old cornflakes.

"Come on, Nathan," said Naomi's mum.

Nathan shut his mouth tight and let cornflake mush dribble down his chin.

"How about feeding him like an airplane?" I suggested. "My baby brother Hank likes it when I do that. Here, I'll show you."

I took the spoon, filled it with flakes, and then let my arm zoom through the air above Nathan's head.

"Here's a loaded jumbo jet coming in to land," I said and made very loud airplane noises.

Nathan opened his mouth in astonishment and I shoved the spoon in quick.

"Unloading bay in operation," I said, and I unhooked the empty spoon from his gums.

"Come on then, Nathan, gobble gobble, while I go looking for the next airplane. Hey, how about a Concorde this time?"

Nathan chewed obediently while I reloaded the spoon and held it at the right Concorde angle. I revved up my sound system.

Unfortunately, my dear non-relative Uncle Mack was revving up his own sound system. After one last bellow he came charging like a bull across the breakfast room.

I landed Concorde, unloaded the new cargo of cornflakes inside Nathan, and tried turning the spoon into a bomber plane with mega-quick, whizz-bang missiles.

Mack certainly exploded. But not in the way I wanted.

"How dare you make this ridiculous noise and bother these poor people," he roared, yanking me up from the table.

"Oh no, she's been no bother at all," said Naomi's mum quickly. "So Elsa's your daughter?"

"No!" I said.

"No!" Mack said.

It was about the only thing we ever agreed on.

"Elsa is my stepdaughter," said Mack. He said the word "step" as if it was some disgusting swear word. "I've done my best to bring her up as if she was my own, but she gets right out of hand sometimes."

I wished I was out of his hand at that precise moment. He was holding me by the shoulders, his fingers digging in hard.

"Well, she's been a very good girl with us, helping me keep my family in order," said Naomi's mum.

"Yes, she got my baby brother Nathan to eat up all his cornflakes," said Naomi.

"It is a pity she can't help out with her own brother and sister," said Mack. "Come on, Elsa, your mum needs you."

He gave a jerk and a pull. I had to go with him or else get my arm torn off. I looked back at Naomi.

"The Cursed Werewolf!" I mouthed, nodding at Mack.

Naomi nodded, grinning at me sympathetically.

I needed sympathy. Mack was in a foul mood.

"What do you think you're doing, rushing around yelling your head off?" he yelled, rushing around.

I could sense it wasn't quite the right time to point out that I was only following my step-daddy's example. He sat me down at our table and started giving me this very old lecture about learning to do as I was told. Pippa started fidgeting and shifting about on her chair as if she were the one getting the lecture, not me.

"I need to go to the toilet," she announced.

"Well, off you go then," said Mack.

"I can't find it by myself," said Pippa.

"I'll take her," I said, jumping at the chance.

I clutched Pippa's hand and escaped the Werewolf's curses. Some of the boys were back in the hall, writing more rude words on the walls. An old lady with a Hoover vacuum cleaner rounded a corner and saw what they were up to.

"Here, you clean that off, you little varmints," she yelled, aiming her vacuum at them.

They laughed and said the words to her.

"Dirty beasts," said the Hoover lady.

She saw us staring.

"Cover your ears up, girls. And you'd better close your eyes too. These little whatsits are destroying this hotel. Destroying it, that's what

they're doing." She banged up against the boys with the vacuum, running the suction nozzle up and down the nearest kid's clothes.

"Stop it, will you! My mum's only just bought me this," he yelled indignantly.

"I'm just trying to clean you up, laddie. Get some of the dirt off you. Now clear off, all of you, or I'll call the Manager."

They straggled away while she held her vacuum aloft in victory. Pippa and I giggled. Mrs. Hoover followed us into the Ladies' Room so she could have a quick smoke.

"Dear oh dear, this place will be the death of

me," she said, lighting up. She tucked her ciggies* and matches back in her pocket and flexed her legs in her baggy old trousers. "It used to be a really classy establishment back in the old days. A really nice business hotel. You could get fantastic tips and everyone spoke to you ever so pleasant. Now you just get a mouthful of abuse. They're all scum that stay here now. Absolute scum."

She said this very fiercely and then blinked a bit at me. "No offense meant, dearie. You seem very nice little girls, you and your sister."

"Aren't we just a bit scummy round the edges?" I said.

"You what? Oh, stop it!" She puffed on her cigarette, chuckling.

"What's scum?" said Pippa, emerging from the toilet and going to wash her hands.

"That's scum," I said, wiping my finger round the edge of the grey sink.

"Now dear, don't shame me. I used to keep this place so clean you could eat your dinner out of one of them sinks. But now I just lose heart.

*ciggies Short for cigarettes. Everyone smokes like a chimney in the hotel so it smells horrid. I say ciggies, you say smokes.

And the management's so cheap, they keep cutting down the staff. How can I keep this place spick and span, eh, especially with my bad legs?" She patted at her trousers and shook her head. Then she glanced again at the sink. "Look, that's a footprint, isn't it? Dear goodness, can you believe it? They're actually putting their feet in the basins now."

"I wonder who on earth that could be," I said, winking at Pippa.

"I know!" said Pippa, not understanding my meaningful wink.

"No you don't," I said quickly.

"Here, we could help you do some cleaning if you like, Pippa and me. I'm good at vacuuming. It's fun."

I wasn't in any hurry to get back to the breakfast room and Mack. I wanted him to cool down a bit first. So Mrs. Hoover sat stiffly on the stairs and did a bit of dusting and Pippa puttered about with a dustpan and brush while I switched on the vacuum and sucked up all the dust on the shabby carpet. I kept imagining

Mack was standing right in front of me. I'd charge at him and knock him flying and then get out a really giant suction nozzle. I wouldn't just snag his clothes, *oh* no. I'd vacuum him right out of existence.

I was galloping along the corridor, laughing fit to bust, when the real Mack suddenly came round the corner. He didn't look very cool at all. He looked as if he might very well be at boiling point.

"What the heck are you playing at, Elsa?"

"I'm not playing, I'm helping do the housework."

"Switch it off! And don't answer me back like that," Mack said. "We thought you both got lost. You've been gone nearly half an hour. Didn't you realize you'd be worrying your mum? Elsa!"

"I thought you didn't want me to answer you," I said.

Mack took a step nearer to me, breathing fire.

"Don't be cross with the kiddie, she's been ever such a help," said Mrs. Hoover. "She's really vacuumed this carpet, I'm telling you. And the little one's been sweeping the stairs, haven't you, pet?"

"Yes, well, I'll thank you to mind your own business," said Mack, snatching Pippa up into his arms. "You come with Daddy, ma chook. We've

been worried sick, wondering what had happened to you. Mum's been up to our room and back, thinking you'd gone up there."

Mack stomped round the corner, still clutching Pippa, and tripped right over the gang of giggling boys writing more dirty words on the wall.

"Get out of my way, you kids," Mack thundered.

Pippa peered at the words from her new vantage point. She stared at the worst word of all. She remembered. She said it loudly and clearly.

"What did you say, Pippa?" said Mack, so taken aback he nearly dropped her.

So she said it again. Unmistakably.

"I'm reading, Dad," she said proudly.

The boys absolutely cracked up at this, snickering and spluttering.

"I'll wipe the smile off your silly faces!" Mack shouted, practically frothing at the mouth. "How dare you write mucky words on the wall so that my little girl learns dirt like that?"

They stopped snickering and started scattering, seeing that Mack meant business. Mack caught hold of one of them, the boy I'd made the face at. He was making faces again now, trying to wriggle free.

"It wasn't me that wrote that word, honest!" he yelled. "It was her."

He pointed to me. All his pals stopped and pointed to me too.

"Yes, it was that girl."

"Yes, that one with all the hair."

"Yeah, that little girl with the loud voice."

It looked like I was in BIG TROUBLE.

I was.

I tried to explain but Mack wouldn't listen.

He hit. And I hurt.

# Chapter 5

## Sweets for Treats

Mack stayed in a horrible mood all that day. All that *week*. And Mum wasn't much better. She didn't get mad at me and shout. She didn't say very much at all. She did a lot of that sitting on the bed and staring into space. Sometimes Mack could snap her out of it. Sometimes he couldn't.

I hated to see Mum all sad and sulky like that. I tried telling her jokes to cheer her up a bit.

"Hey Mum, what's ten meters tall and green and sits in the corner?"

"Oh Elsa, please. Just leave me be."

"The Incredible Sulk!"

I really laughed. But Mum didn't even smile.

"OK, try this one. Why did the biscuit* cry?"

"What biscuit? What are you talking about?"

"Any biscuit."

"Can I have a biscuit, Mum?" said Pippa.

"Look, just listen to the *joke*. Why did the biscuit cry, eh? Because his mother was a wafer so long."

I paused. Nobody reacted.

"Don't you get it?"

"Just give it a rest, Elsa, please," Mum said, and she lay back on her bed and buried her head under the pillow.

I stared at Mum worriedly. I so badly wanted her to cheer up.

"Mum? Mum." I went over to her and shook her arm.

"Leave her be," said Mack.

I took no notice.

*biscuit A small flat sweet cake. I say biscuit, you say cookie. English biscuits are usually smaller than American cookies. It's not fair!

"Mum, what happened to the lady who slept with her head under the pillow?"

Mum groaned.

"When she woke up she found the fairies had taken all her teeth out!"

Mum didn't twitch.

"Elsa, I'm telling you. Leave her alone," Mack growled.

I tried just one more.

"Are you going to sleep, Mum? Listen, what happened to the lady who dreamed she was eating a huge great marshmallow?"

"Can I have a marshmallow?" said Pippa.

"When she woke up her pillow had disappeared!"

Mum didn't move. But Mack did.

"I'm warning you, Elsa. Just one more of your stupid jokes and you've had it!"

"Dad, can I have some biscuits or some sweets or something? I'm hungry," Pippa whined.

"OK, OK." Mack fumbled in his pocket for change. "Take her down to that shop on the corner, Elsa. Here."

"What do baby ghosts like chewing? Booble gum!"

"I thought I told you. NO MORE JOKES!"

"OK, OK." I grabbed Pippa and scooted out

of the room.

"Why are adults boring?" I asked her, as we went down the stairs. "Because they're groan-ups."

I roared with laughter. I'm not altogether sure Pippa understood, but she laughed to keep me company. The big bunny lady in reception put her pointy finger to her lips and went "Sh! Sh!" at us.

"She sounds like a train," I said to Pippa. "Hey, what do you call a train full of toffee?"

"Oh, toffee! Are you buying toffee? I like toffee too."

"No, Pippa, you're not concentrating. What do you call a train full of toffee? A chew-chew train."

Pippa blinked up at me blankly. I laughed. She laughed too, but she was just copying me like she always does. I wished she was old enough to appreciate my jokes. I longed to try them all out on Naomi, but she was at school.

That was one of the advantages of going to live at the O Yal Htl. I couldn't go to my old school because it was miles and miles away. No one had said anything about going to any other school. I certainly wasn't going to bring the subject up.

I took hold of Pippa's hand and we went out of the hotel and down the road to where there was this one shop selling sweets and ciggies and papers and videos—all the things you need.

Some of the boys from the hotel were messing about at the video stands, whizzing them around too fast and acting out parts from the films. One of them lunged at me, pointing his hands, pretending to be Freddie from Elm Street.

"Ooooh, I'm so fwightened," I said, sighing heavily. "What are you lot doing here, anyway? Are you skipping school?"

They shuffled a bit so I was obviously right.

"Don't you tell on us or you'll get it, see," said another, trying to act dead tough.

"Don't worry. *I* don't tell tales," I said, looking witheringly at the funny-face boy who had told on me.

He shuffled a bit more, his face turning red.

"Yeah, well, I didn't think your dad would get mad at you like that," he said quickly.

"He's not my dad. He's just my mum's husband, that's all."

"Did he hit you? We heard you yelling."

"You'd yell if he was laying into you."

"Here. Have this," said the funny-face boy, and he handed me his big black magic-marker pen, the one I'd used to correct his spelling to write the truly worst word ever.

"Hey, are you giving this to me?" I said.

"Yeah, if you want."

"You bet I want! My own black felt-tip's run out. Hey, what goes black and white, black and white, black and white?"

"Hmm?" he said, looking blank.

But one of his mates spoilt it.

"A penguin rolling down a hill," he said, grinning. "That's an *old* joke."

"OK, OK, what's black and white and red all over?"

I paused. This time I'd got them.

"A sunburnt penguin!"

Funny-face suddenly snorted with laughter. The others all snickered too. Laughing at my joke! I'd have happily stood there cracking jokes all day but the man behind the counter started to get annoyed so the boys slunk off while Pippa and I chose our sweets. It took a long time, especially as Pippa kept choosing and changing. Once or twice she changed her mind *after* she'd had a little experimental lick of a licorice stick or a red jelly spider but the man behind the counter couldn't see down far enough to spot her.

We ended up with:

We ate them on the way back to the hotel. We weren't in any hurry to get back. Mack had been so grouchy recently he'd even gotten mad at Pippa.

I meant to save a chocolate bar for Naomi, and a toffee chew or two for her brothers, but I seemed to be ever so hungry somehow, and by the time Naomi got back from school there were just a few dolly mixtures left (and they were a bit dusty and sticky because Pippa had been "feed-ing" them to Baby Pillow half the afternoon).

"Never mind, I'll give them a little wash," said Naomi, going into the Ladies' Room.

She and I scrunched up together on the win-dowsill, feet propped on the sink, and we read the worst parts of her Cursed Werewolf book and got the giggles. My Pippa and her Nicky and Neil and Nathan kept on bothering us so we filled the other sinks with water and hauled the little kids up so they could have a paddle. They were only supposed to dangle their feet. They dangled quite a bit more.

I was scared I'd get into trouble with Mum and Mack for getting Pippa soaked, but luckily Mum didn't notice and Mack had gone out for a takeaway and taken Hank with him. Hank loves to go anywhere with Mack. He's a really weird baby. He thinks his dad is great.

I think Mack is great too. A great big hairy warthog.

Pippa and Nicky and Neil and Nathan weren't the only ones who got soaked when they went paddling in the sinks. The floor in the Ladies' Room turned into a sort of sea. Naomi and I tried to mop it up but we only had loo paper to do it with so we weren't very successful.

Mrs. Hoover had to mop it up and she wasn't very pleased. I felt bad about it so the next day Pippa and I helped her with her vacuuming. I'd got stuck with Hank as well, but I tried hard to get him to flick a duster. He seemed determined to use it as a cuddle blanket but Mrs. Hoover didn't mind.

"Oh, what a little sweetie! Bless him!" she cooed.

"Have you got some sweeties?" Pippa asked hopefully.

"You're just like my little granddaughter, pet. Always asking her grandma for sweeties. Here you are, then." Mrs. Hoover gave us both a fruit drop. Hank had to make do with chewing his dust rag, because he might swallow the fruit drop whole and choke.

"Yum yum, I've got an orange. I like them best. I like the red bestest of all," said Pippa hopefully.

I frowned at her but Mrs. Hoover laughed.

"You're a greedy little madam," she said, handing over a raspberry drop too.

"What do you say, Pippa?" I said.

"Thank you ever so much Mrs. Hoover."

"What?" said Mrs. Hoover, because Mrs. Hoover wasn't her real name at all, it was just our name for her. Her real name was Mrs. Macpherson but I didn't like calling her that because it reminded me too much of my Mack Person. My least favorite person of all time.

He'd given me another smack because Pippa and I were playing hunt the magic marble in our room and I'd hidden it under the rug covering the torn part of the carpet. How was I to know that Mack would burst back

from playing cards with his mates and stomp across the rug and skid on the marble and go flying?

I couldn't help laughing. He really did look hilarious. Especially when he landed bonk on his bum.

"I'll teach you not to laugh at me!" he said, scrambling to get up.

He did his best.

But I had the last laugh. I slipped off into the Ladies' Room all by myself and had a little fun with my new black magic-marker pen.

# Chapter 6

I soon got into a Royal Hotel routine. I always woke up early. I'd scrunch up in bed with my flashlight and my joke books and wise up on a few more wisecracks. I'd tell the jokes over and over until I knew them by heart. I'd often roll around laughing myself.

Sometimes I shook the bed so much Pippa woke up wondering if she was in the middle of an earthquake. If I caused earthquakes Pippa was likely to cause her own natural disasters. Floods.

Mum kept getting mad at her and saying she was much too big to be wetting the bed and she didn't let Pippa have anything to drink at teatime but it still didn't make much difference. Pippa cried because she was so thirsty and she *still* wet the bed more often than not.

So another of my little routines was to sneak all Pippa's wet bedclothes down to the laundry room before Mum and Mack woke up. There were only two washing machines and one dryer. You usually couldn't get near them. But early in the morning everyone was either fast asleep or getting the kids ready for school so there was a good chance I could wash the sheets out for my leaky little sister.

The only other people around were some of the Asian ladies in their pretty clothes. They looked like people out of fairy tales instead of ordinary mums in boring old T-shirts and leggings.

They sounded as if they were saying strange and secret things too as they whispered together in their own language. Some of their children could speak good English even though they'd only been over here a few months, but the mums didn't bother. They generally just stuck in a little clump together.

I felt a little shy with them at first and I think they felt shy with me too. But after a few encounters in the laundry room we started to nod to each other. One time they'd run out of washing powder so I gave them a few sprinkles of ours. The next day they gave me half a packet back *and* a special pink sweet. It was the sweetest sweet I've ever eaten in my life. It was so sweet it started to get sickly, and when I got back to room 608 I passed it on to Pippa. She enjoyed it hugely for a while but it finally got the better of her too. We rubbed a little on Hank's pacifier and it kept him quiet half the morning.

Keeping Hank quiet was a big job at the hotel. He'd always been a happy sort of baby, even if he did act like a bit of a thug at times, bashing about with his fat fists and kicking hard with his bootees. But he'd never really whined and whimpered that much. Now he didn't seem to do much else. It was probably because he was so cooped up. He was just getting to the stage when he wanted to crawl around all over the place and explore. But he couldn't really crawl in room 608. It was much too little and crowded.

It was dangerous too. If you took your eye off him for two seconds he'd be doing this

or this

or this.

There was only one way to keep him out of mischief.

He didn't like it one little bit. He wanted to be up and about.

Mum and Mack didn't want to be up and about at all. They just wanted to sleep in. Most days they even stopped bothering to go down to breakfast. So Pippa and Hank and I had our breakfast and then we helped Mrs. Hoover and then we played about in the hall. We set Hank down at one end and raced to the other end and had a very quick game before he caught up with us.

Hank got so good at crawling he could probably have won a gold medal at the Baby Olympics. If we wanted any peace at  all we had to change his crawling track into an obstacle race.

Sometimes we collected several babies and had a race. The other brothers and sisters placed bets. That was good. Pippa and I made lots of money because Hank always won.

We got pretty noisy and sometimes Mack would come staggering out and tell us all to pipe down. He'd yell if he was in a bad mood but he didn't frighten anyone now. The kids just muttered amongst themselves about pimply bums and brain transplants and cracked up laughing. All the girls had read the jokes in the Ladies' Room downstairs. Even some of the boys had dashed in and out for a dare.

Mack and Mum often didn't really get up until lunchtime. Lunch was my favorite meal of the day because I could go along to the shop on the corner and choose it. I had to make sure I bought the *Sun* for Mack, and maybe something boring like a carton of milk or a packet of biscuits—but then I could buy crisps* and Coke and chocolates and sweets and anything else I wanted with the money left over. Pippa and I always had a Mega-Feast.

## SAMPLE WEEK'S MENU
## OF THE MEGA-FEAST

*Monday:* Apple juice, Mini Cheddars, Toffee Crisp, Woppa

*Tuesday:* Strawberry Ribena, Californian corn chips, Cadbury's Flake, Buster bar

*Wednesday:* Lucozade, Chicken Tikka Hula Hoops, Bounty, Flying Saucers

*Thursday:* Dr. Pepper drink, Chipsticks, Galaxy, Sherbet Fountain

*Friday:* Coke, Salt-and-vinegar crisps, Crunchie, Fizz cola-bottle sweets

*Saturday:* Strawberry Break Time Milk, Pork rinds, Picnic, Dolly-beads

*Sunday:* Lilt, Skips (chili flavor), Fruit-and-nut chocolate, Giant Licorice

*crisps Very thin fried sliced potato, eaten cold. They come in all sorts of wacky flavors: prawn, smoky bacon, curried beef. I say crisps, you say potato chips.

This is all times two, because Pippa always copied me. Hank generally wanted a lick here and a munch there after he'd had his bottle and his baby food, but there was still heaps left for us.

We sometimes went out in the afternoons. Once we went to the park.

I liked it best of all when Mack went off with his mates and took Hank along too and Mum and Pippa and me went to the shops. Not the shop on the corner. Not the Kwik-Save or the betting shop or the chip shop down the road. The real shops in town. Especially the Flowerfields Shopping Center. It's this great glass shopping

mall with real flowers blossoming in big bouquets
all around the entrance, and painted flowers
climbing over the door of each individual shop,
and there are lovely ladies wandering round in
long dresses who hand you a flower for free.

Mum and Pippa and I could spend hours and
hours and hours wandering round the
Flowerfields Shopping Center.

Of course we couldn't ever buy the books or
the tapes or the toys or the outfits. But we could
go back the next day and the next and read and
listen and play and try them on all over again.

And then when we had to trail all the way back to the O yal Htl and we were all tired and we didn't even have the money for the bus, we could still smell our flowers and  pretend they were big bouquets.

I made up this story to myself that I was a famous comedienne and I'd just done this amazingly funny routine on stage and everyone had

laughed and laughed and then they'd clapped and clapped and begged for an encore and showered me with roses ...

"Hey, Mum, Pippa, what do you get if you cross a rose with a python?"

"Oh Elsa, please, give it a rest."

"I don't know what you get—but don't try to smell it!" I laughed. Then I tried again.

"What did one rose say to the other rose?"

"'Hello, Rose,'" said Pippa. She laughed. "Hey, I said the joke!"

"Don't you start too," Mum groaned.

"That's not a joke, Pippa. It's not funny. No, *listen*. What did one rose say to the other rose? It said, 'Hi, Bud.' See? *That's* funny."

"No, it's not," said Mum.

I ignored her.

"All right then. What did the bee say to the flower?"

"'Hi, Flower?'" said Pippa. "Is that right? Have I said the joke now?"

"No! Pippa, you can't just say any old thing. It's got to be a joke. Now, what did the bee say to the flower? It said, 'Hello honey.'"

"And I'm going to say 'Goodbye Sweetie' if you dare come out with one more of your daft jokes," said Mum, but she didn't really mean it. She was just joking herself.

Mum could still be a lot of fun, especially going round Flowerfields, but when we got back to room 608 she wilted like the flowers.

We spent the evenings indoors. So did everyone else around us. The people in room 607 had more arguments. The people in 609 still had their telly blaring. The people underneath in room 508 still played their heavy-metal music. You could feel our room vibrating with the noise.

We tried going downstairs to the television lounge. Well, that was a laugh. There wasn't anywhere to lounge, like a sofa or a comfy armchair. There were just these old vinyl straight-back chairs, the same sort as in the breakfast room, but even older, so you had to play musical chairs finding the ones without the wobbly legs. There wasn't much of a television either. It was supposed to be color but the switch wouldn't stay stable, so people's faces were gloomy gray and then suddenly blushed bright scarlet for no reason. There was something wrong with the sound too. It was all blurry and every time anyone talked there was a buzzing sound.

"I'm starting to feel that way myself," said Mum, putting her hands over her ears.

"Don't get all moody, for goodness sake," said Mack. "I can't stand this. I'm going out."

Mum hunched up even smaller in her chair after he'd gone. I went over to her and tried putting my arm round her. She didn't seem to notice.

"Good riddance to bad rubbish," I said fiercely.

We both knew where he'd gone. Down to the pub. He'd drink all our money and then try to scrounge from some mates. And then he'd come staggering back and be all stupid and snore all night and in the morning he'd have such a sore head he'd snap at the least thing.

I got ten out of ten for an accurate prediction. But by the afternoon he was acting sorry. He'd won a bet so he took Mum out in the evening while I babysat and then on Sunday morning he got up ever so early. I heard him go out before anyone else was awake. I couldn't help hoping he was sneaking off for good. But he came back at ten o'clock, staggering again, but this time it was because he was carrying a television.

"I got it for cheap at a sale," he said triumphantly. "There! Now we don't have to sit in that stupid lounge. We can watch our own telly. Great, eh?"

It wasn't a color television, just a little old black-and-white portable set. It took ages to retune it when you changed channels, and of course you couldn't get cable. But it was our *own* television. We could put the sound up so loud you could hardly hear the arguments in 607 and if we tuned into the same program as the people in 609 it was like we were listening in stereo.

Mum didn't get so droopy now that she had television to watch. She switched it on as soon as she woke up and it was still on long after I settled down to sleep. I liked to listen to it as I snuggled under the covers. But sometimes I put my head right down under my blanket and put my hands hard over my ears so that they made their own odd roaring noise and then I switched on this tiny private little television inside my own head. It was much better than the real thing because I could make up all my own programs.

I was the lady on breakfast television interviewing people in my bedroom

and I was in all the soaps

and I won all the quizzes

and the wrestling

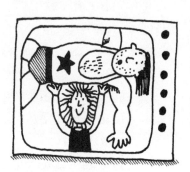

and I was in a show
for kids

and I was in lots of
films

and best of all I had
my very own comedy
show and it was a
huge success.

# Chapter 7

One Slurpy Square of Yorkie Bar

Just when I'd gotten into this happy little routine at the Royal, Mum went and messed it all up. She stopped drooping. She started dashing about. She said we weren't going to be stuck in this crummy bed-and-breakfast dump a day longer. She went to the housing department and the Social Services. She armed herself with Hank and Pippa and me, and whenever we were stuck too long in a queue she sent Pippa and me off sniping into enemy territory in search of a toilet and she hoped Hank would howl. He was our best weapon, like an exploding hand grenade, a great way of getting to the front quickly.

Mum went into battle day after day, but it didn't make any difference. We had to stay put because there wasn't anywhere else for us to go. But someone at Social Services told Mum about this drop-in center where the kids could play and you got cheap food, so Mum thought she'd give it a go.

I didn't like the sound of it.

It wasn't that bad actually, just this big room, half of it for the mums and half for the kids. It was pretty crowded in the nursery and there was just this one woman going crackers trying to keep all the kids happy.

Pippa and I helped a little.

But then someone from the Social Services came and said the center had to be closed because there wasn't any more money to fund it. Mum started moaning and complaining, saying this drop-in center was practically saving her life because we were stuck in a shelter hotel and it was no place for little kids. The Social Services person got a bit nervous because Mum can get ever so fierce when she feels like it, and he promised to put Hank's name down on the day nursery waiting list.

"Oh, very funny," said Mum. "He'll be twenty-one before he gets a place."

"This little girly here will be old enough for school soon," he said, timidly patting Pippa.

Then he turned to me.

Oh-oh. I should have seen it coming.

"Why isn't this girl in school, hmm? Now, I *can* help you here. We'll get her registered at the local school right away and she can start on Monday morning."

Thanks a lot.

It had been the one ultra big bonus of life at the O yal Htl. NO SCHOOL.

I knew Naomi and Funny-Face and most of the other kids at the hotel had to go. I'd hoped nobody had noticed I wasn't there. I don't like school. Well, my first school was OK. There was a smiley teacher and we could play with pink dough and we all got to sing these soppy old nursery rhymes. I could sing loudest and longest.

But then we moved up to Scotland and I had to go to a new school and it was all different and I got teased because of the way I talk. Then we moved back down South and lived in the apartment and that school was the sort where even the little kids get their heads held down the toilet. It was a pretty grim way of getting your hair washed. I hated that school. But then the next one, my last school, wasn't so bad. That was when we were living in the lovely house and we were almost an ordinary family and even Mack didn't smack. Well, not so much.

It was a bit depressing though. They gave me all these tests and stuff and I couldn't do a lot of it. They thought I was thick. *I* thought I was thick. I had to go to these extra classes to help me with my reading and my writing and my math. The other kids laughed at me.

I like it when people laugh at my jokes. But I can't stand it when they laugh at *me.*

But I had this really great remedial teacher, Mr. Jamieson, only everyone called him Jamie, even us kids. He was very gentle and he didn't yell at you when you couldn't do something. He worked with me and whenever I learnt the least little thing he smiled and stuck his thumb up and said I was doing really fine. So I *felt* fine and I learnt a lot more and then Jamie got me to do some other tests

and it turned out I wasn't thick at all. I was INTELLIGENT.

Jamie asked me about all the other schools and he said that it was no wonder I hadn't been able to learn much, because I'd had so many changes. But now I could get settled in and swoop through all the stuff I didn't know and Jamie said I'd soon end up at the top of the class, not the bottom. So there.

But then Mack lost his job and we lost our house and we ended up in the O yal Htl, miles and miles and miles away from my old school.

Still, if I had to go to school, that was the one I wanted to go to. So I could still see Jamie.

"Of course you can't go, Elsa," Mum said. "You'd have to take two buses. And then walk miles. We can't afford the fares. And you'd wear out your trainers in weeks. No, you're to go to this Mayberry School where the other kids go."

Only they didn't all go, of course. Naomi went. The Asian kids went. One or two others. But Funny-Face and nearly all the boys cut school every day.

I decided that's what I'd do. I might know I was intelligent, but this school might give me the wrong sort of tests. I could easily end up being thought thick all over again. There was no guarantee at all I'd find another Jamie.

I started hanging around more with Funny-Face and the others. I had to work hard to get them to like me. I had to tell them lots and lots of jokes. They soon got sick of my usual repertoire. Get that fancy word. I'm *not* thick. I know lots and lots of things, though they're not usually the sort of things they like you to know in school. All comedians have to have a repertoire—it's all the jokes in their act. So to impress Funny-Face and his Famous Five followers I had to tell a few rude jokes. Naughty jokes. Blue jokes. Dirty jokes. You know the kind.

The trouble was that Pippa still hung round me most of the time, and she heard some of the jokes too. I told her and told her and *told* her that she mustn't repeat them, but one time she forgot. She told Mack.

And then guess what. SMACK.

"It wasn't my fault this time," said Funny-Face afterwards.

"It was my fault," said Pippa, and she burst into tears.

"You didn't mean to," I said, giving her a cuddle. "Here, don't cry, you soppy little thing. It's me he smacked, not you."

"You don't hardly ever cry," said Pippa.

"She's tough," said Funny-Face, and he sounded admiring.

"Yeah, that's me. Tough as old boots," I said, swaggering.

So on the Monday I was due to start school I set off with Naomi, but the minute we got down the road I veered off with Funny-Face and the Famous Five.

"Hey, Elsa. Why don't you come with me?" Naomi said, looking disappointed. "I thought we were friends. Why do you want to go off with all the boys?"

"We are friends, Naomi. Course we are. I just don't want to go to this dopey old school, that's all. I'll see you later, same as usual, and we'll play together and have fun."

"But it isn't a dopey school, really. And I hoped we'd get to be in the same class. I even swapped desks with this other girl so there'd be a place for you to sit beside me."

"Oh Naomi," I said, fidgeting. She was starting to make me feel bad. But I really didn't want to go to school. I didn't even want to be in Naomi's class and sit beside her. Naomi looked like she was really brainy, being a bookworm and all that. I knew I was intelligent, Jamie said so, but I hadn't quite caught up with all the things I'd missed, and maybe it would still look as if I was thick. I didn't want Naomi knowing.

So I went off with Funny-Face and the others. I hung around with them all day long. It was OK for a while. We couldn't hang about the hotel or risk going round the town because someone would spot us and guess we were cutting, but we went to this camp place they'd made on a demolition site. It wasn't much of a camp, just some corrugated iron shoved together with a blue tarpaulin for a roof. It was pretty crowded when we were all crammed in there knee-to-knee, and there was nothing to sit on, just cold rough ground.

"Well, you could make it more comfortable,

couldn't you?" said Funny-Face.

"Yeah, you fix it up for us, Elsa," said one of his mates.

"Why me?" I said indignantly.

"You're a girl, aren't you?"

I snorted. I wasn't going along with that sort of sexist rubbish. They seemed to think they were Peter Pan and the Lost Boys and I was little Wendy.

"Catch me doing all your donkey work," I said. "Hey, what do you get if you cross a zebra and a donkey? A zee donk. And what do you get if you cross a pig and a zebra? Striped sausages." I kept firing jokes at them as the resident entertainer, and so they stopped expecting me to be the chief cook and bottlewasher.

They started bullying the littlest boy, a runny-nosed kid not much older than Pippa, getting him to run around the site finding sacks and stuff for us to sit on. He tripped over a brick and cut both his knees and got more runny-nosed than ever, so I mopped him up and told him a few more jokes to make him laugh. It wasn't easy. His name was Simon and he certainly seemed a bit simple. But he was a brave little kid and so I stuck up for him when the boys were bossing him around and when we were all squatting on our makeshift cushions and Funny-Face started passing round a crumpled packet of cigarettes, I wouldn't let Simon sample a smoke.

"You don't want to mess around with ciggies, my lad, they'll stunt your growth," I said firmly, and gave him a toffee chew instead.

I didn't smoke either. I can't stand the smell and they make me dizzy. But even though Simon and I didn't participate in the smoking session it still got so foggy in the camp my head started reeling. It came as a relief when the blue tarpaulin suddenly got ripped right off and we were exposed by this other dopey gang of boys also cutting school. They threw a whole pile of dust and dirt all over us as we sat there gasping, and then they ran away screeching with laughter.

So then, of course, Funny-Face and the Famous Five started breathing fire instead of

inhaling it, and they went rampag-
ing across the demolition site to get
their revenge. I rampaged a bit too,
but it all seemed silly to me. There
was a sort of war with both gangs
throwing stones rather wildly.
Simon got overexcited and wouldn't
keep down out of range, so he got hit on the head.

It was only a little bump but it frightened him
and he started yelling. The boys just stood
around laughing at him, though they looked a bit
shamefaced. So I rushed over to him going "Mee-
Maa Mee-Maa Mee-Maa" like an ambulance, and
then I made a big production of examining him
and pretending his whole head had been knocked
off and he needed a major operation. Simon was
so simple he believed me at first and started crying harder, but when he figured out it was all a
joke he started to enjoy being the center of atten-
tion as a major casualty of war.

The war seemed to have fizzled out anyway,
and the rival gang wandered off down to the chip
shop because it was nearly lunchtime.

That proved to be a major drawback to cutting
school. None of us lot had any lunch. We didn't
have any spare cash either. As Social Services
kids we were entitled to a free school lunch but

they just issued you with a ticket, not actual cash you could spend. So because we weren't at school we were stuck. I began to wish I hadn't been so generous with my toffee chew.

One of the boys found half a Yorkie bar he'd forgotten about right at the bottom of his bomber-jacket pocket. The wrapping paper had disintegrated and the chocolate was liberally sprinkled with little fluffy bits and after he'd passed it round for everyone to nibble it was all slurpy with boy-lick too—but it was food, after all, so I ate a square.

I was starving all afternoon and getting pretty bored with cutting school. I had to keep an eye on the time so I would go back to the O yal Htl at the same time I would have been let out of school. When you keep on looking at the time it goes very s-l-o-w-l-y. Half a century seemed to plod past when it had only been half an hour.

But e-v-e-n-t-u-a-l-l-y it was time to be making tracks. And then I found out I'd been wasting my time after all. Mum had decided to trot down to the school with Hank and Pippa to see how I'd gotten along on my first day. Only I wasn't there, obviously, so she went into the school to find me and of course the teacher said I hadn't ever arrived.

Mum was MAAAAAAAAAD.

And then Mack got in on the act and you can guess what he did.

So I stormed off in a huff down the corridor.

I sat there all by myself and it hurt where Mack had hit me and my tummy rumbled and I felt seriously fed up. But I didn't cry.

And then I heard footsteps. The clacky-stomp of high heels. Mum had come to find me. I thought at first she might still be mad, but she sat right down beside me, even though she nearly split her leggings, and she put her arms round me. I did cry a little then.

"I'm sorry, sausage," she said, nuzzling into my wild lion's mane. "I know he's too hard on you sometimes.

"But it's just that you won't do as you're told. And you've got to go to school, Elsa."

"It's not fair. I don't want to go to that rotten old school where I don't know anyone."

"You know that nice Naomi. She's your friend! Oh, come on now, Elsa, you're never *shy*. You!" Mum laughed and tweaked my nose.

"The others all cut. The boys."

"I don't care about them. I care about you. My girl. Now listen. You don't want to go to school. *I* don't want you to go to school. I'd much sooner have you around the hotel keeping the kids quiet for me. I've missed you awfully today."

"Really?" I said, cheering up considerably.

"Yes, but *listen.* You've *got* to go to school because it's the law, see, and if you don't go they can say I'm not looking after you properly. You know the Social Services people are always checking on us as it is. We don't want to give them any excuse whatsoever to whip you into Foster Care."

She'd got me there. So I had to go the next morning. I set off with all the other kids, and when we got to the end of the road, Funny-Face and the Famous Five all called to me.

"Come on then, Elsa."

"Come with us, eh?"

"Come to the camp."

Little Simon even came and held my hand and asked if I'd come and play ambulances with him. His face fell a mile when I had to say no. So I gave him a packet of Polos* and showed him how

*Polos* Little white mints with a hole in the middle. I know a Polo joke: What's furry and minty? A Polo Bear! I say Polos, you say Lifesavers.

to poke his pointy little tongue through the hole. That cheered him up a lot.

"Elsa! Why aren't you coming?" said Funny-Face. "You chicken or something?"

"Hey, what would you see at the chicken show? Hen-tertainment."

"That is a fowl joke," said Funny-Face.

We both cracked up.

"Come on. You can be good fun . . . for a girl," said Funny-Face.

"You can be quite perceptive . . . for a boy," I said, and I waved to him and walked off with Naomi.

"Is he your boyfriend then?" she said.

"Look, *I'm* the one that's meant to make the jokes," I said. "Him!"

"He likes you all the same," said Naomi. "You and him will be slinking off to room one hundred and ten soon."

"Naomi!" I nudged her and she nudged me back and we both fell over giggling.

The Manager and the bunny lady can't rent room 110 because it's so damp all the wallpaper's peeled off and the Health Inspector's been around. But someone stole a spare key and some of the big kids pair off, boy and girl, and sneak into the empty room together. They don't seem to mind the dampness.

But catch me going anywhere with Funny-Face. Least of all room 110.

Naomi and I had a laugh about it, like I said, but as I got nearer and nearer to school there suddenly didn't seem anything to laugh at.

"Cheer up, Elsa. It's OK, really it is. Look, tell me a school joke."

I swallowed. My mouth had suddenly gone dry. For once I didn't really feel in a jokey mood. Still, a comedienne has to be funny no matter what she feels like.

"OK, so there's this geography teacher, right, and he's asking all the kids where all these mountains are, and he says to the little thick one, 'Where are the Andes?' and the little thick one blinks a bit and then pipes up, 'At the end of my armies.'"

My own andies were cold and clenched tight. I felt like the little thick one, all right.

# Chapter 8

I was right to feel edgy. I didn't like this new school at all.

I didn't get to sit next to Naomi in her class. I was put in the special class, which was really  humiliating for a start. They said it was just for a little while, to see how things worked out. Hmm. Fine if they did work out. But what if they didn't? Where do you go if you're too thick even for the special class? Do they march you right back to nursery school?

I didn't like my teacher in this strange class I got stuck in.

I wanted a young man teacher like Jamie. Mrs. Fisher was old and probably a woman (though she had a moustache above her upper lip). She also had a hard voice that could rip right through you, though when I first got shoved in her class she stretched her thin lips in a smile and said in ever such sugary, sweetie tones that she was pleased to meet me, and oh what a pretty name Elsa is, and here was my notebook and have this nice sharp pencil, dearie, and why don't you sit at the front where I can see you and write me a little story about yourself.

She was trying to pretend she was really interested in me, but she couldn't fool me. When she took us all out in the playground to have P.E., she got talking to one of the other teachers. The other teacher saw me and asked Mrs. Fisher who I was. Mrs. Fisher didn't even tell her my name. She just said: "Oh, that's just one of the shelter children."

I'm not even a she. I'm a That. Some sort of boring blob who doesn't have a name, who doesn't even have a sex.

Elsa the Blob. Hey, I kind of like that idea. I could be a great big giant monster Blob and go around obliterating people. Mack is still first on my list but Mrs. Fisher comes a close second.

I wrote her a little story about myself all right. I wrote that my real name is Elsarina and I'm a child star—actress, singer and comedienne—and I've been in lots of ads on the telly and done pantomimes and heaps of musicals, and I was actually currently starring in a traveling repertory performance of *Annie*—me playing Annie, of course. And I wrote that my mum and the rest of my family are all in show biz too, part of the company, and *that's* why we're currently living in a hotel, because we travel around putting on our shows.

I tried to make it sound absolutely true. But when she read it she just gave me one of those smug old smiles.

"This is certainly some story, dear," she said. "Rather a *make-believe* story, I'm afraid."

The other kids tittered, though they didn't know what she was talking about. She handed me my story back with all my spelling and punctuation mistakes underlined. There seemed to be more red ink on the page than pencil.

But I was not deterred. If I was meant to be thick then some of the kids in the class were as dense as drains, and gurgled. So I tried out my Elsarina story on them, and they were all impressed, even the big tough guys. I gave them a few quick samples of my comic routine out on the playground and some of them laughed and then I treated them to a rendition of "The Sun Will Come Out Tomorrow." I forget what a powerful voice I've got. One or two kids ran for cover, but those that stayed seemed to truly appreciate my performance.

School didn't seem quite so bad at this stage. I had my little group of fans who happily drank in everything I told them. I got a bit carried away and started elaborating about my mum being this really beautiful actress and yet she could belt out

a song and dance up a storm in this really classy cabaret act . . . and every so often I seemed to step outside myself and hear my own voice and I could see I was tempting fate telling all these lies. Well, they weren't completely lies. Mum *used* to be beautiful before she met up with Mack and had some more kids so that she lost her lovely figure and gained a few worry lines. She could *still* look beautiful if only she'd bother to slap on some makeup and fix her hair properly. She really used to sing and dance too. She'd sing along to all the records on the radio in a happy husky voice and she'd dance away, wiggling her hips and waggling her fingers. So Mum *could* sing and dance and if only she'd had the right breaks then I'm sure she really could have been a star . . .

All the same, I shut up at lunchtime when I met Naomi. It was great to have my own special friend to wander around the playground with. School lunches weren't so bad either. They weren't as good as my Mega-Feast at home with Pippa, but you were allowed to choose what you wanted, so I had a big plateful of pizza and chips and I got everyone at our lunch table laughing with a whole load of pizza jokes that aren't fit for publication. Even my silly old chip joke went down well salted.

"Hey, what are hot, greasy and romantic? Chips that pass in the night!"

The afternoon wasn't so great because we had to divide up into groups to do all this dumb weighing and measuring. I could do that easy-peasy but I didn't know how you write it all down. I didn't want to admit this so I made a lot of it up, and then of course Mrs. Fisher came nosing around and when she saw all my calculations she sighed and scored a line right through them, so it was obvious to everyone I'd got it all wrong. She sat down with me and tried to explain how to do it. I felt so embarrassed in front of the other kids that I couldn't concentrate on what she was saying. She had to go through the whole thing again, speaking e-v-e-r s-o s-l-o-w-l-y because she obviously thought she had a very thick person on her hands.

The other kids started to snicker by this stage, so when Mrs. Fisher at last left us in peace I had to work hard to regain their respect. I started on about my stage clothes and my mum's stage

clothes and my little sister Pippa's stage clothes, and once I'd started on Pippa I couldn't stop, and soon I'd turned her into this adorable little child star, Pipette, with chubby cheeks and a head of curls and though she hadn't started school yet she could sing and dance like a real little professional.

I was certainly going a bit over the top here, because even Mack and Mum admit that Pippa is plain. Well, the poor kid can't help it, being stuck with Mack as a dad. She hasn't got chubby cheeks, she hasn't got curls (Mum did try with her curling iron once when Pippa was going to a party but her hair ended up looking like it had exploded). She isn't even little—she's nearly as big as me though she's half my age—and as for singing and dancing, well. Pippa can't ever remember the words to any song, let alone the tune, and the only sort of dancing she can do is slam-dancing, though she doesn't *mean* to barge straight into you.

But I built her up into such a little Baby Wonder that the kids in my class were drooling, and they all wanted to see the show with me and this mega-brilliant little brat and our glamorous movie-star mummy.

"Sorry, folks, we've been sold out for weeks because the show's so popular," I said breezily, though my heart was beating fit to bust.

That shut them up for a few seconds, but then I started to wonder about going-home time. Mum had found me out yesterday by coming around to the school. What if she came again today? What if she'd just pulled on her oldest old T-shirt and leggings and hadn't bothered to do her hair? All the children would see her for themselves. And even if I could somehow manage to convince them that she was just practicing for an upcoming searingly realistic drama on the telly about a care-worn young mother ground down by the system, they'd see Pippa too.

It might help matters if my whole family were there. I could tell them that Mack was all set for a remake of King Kong. He didn't even need to

 bother with a costume. I shot out of school the moment the bell rang. It was a huge great relief to see that Mum wasn't there, though I

couldn't help feeling a weeny bit angry all the same, because she *said* she'd come. She wasn't back at the hotel either. None of them were. I couldn't get into room 608 because I didn't have a key, so I had to hang around the halls for ages. Naomi came along but she was irritated with me because I hadn't waited for her after school, and she couldn't play with me now anyway because she had to help her mum with her brothers. Then Funny-Face sloped into view, scuffing his trainers and spitting. He was even more irritated with me because my mum had stirred things up yesterday and the school had checked their records and sent the truant officer around and Funny-Face and the Famous Five had to turn up at school tomorrow or *else*.

"Or else you'll all get into trouble and Elsa'll get into trouble for getting you all into trouble," I said, making a funny face at Funny-Face.

He didn't make one back. He called me a lot of rude names, even the really bad one he wrote on

the wall that I had to correct.

I just walked away and pretended I didn't care. But I felt a bit friendless by now. And I was starting to get very worried that I might be familyless too.

Why had they all gone off without telling me where they were going? What if they'd finally got fed up with me and packed up and left? I knew Mack didn't want me. He'd go off like a shot and he'd take Pippa and Hank because they were his kids and he cared about them. But Mum wouldn't walk out on me, would she? Although only this morning, when something was wrong with the drains and someone else's dirty water came bubbling up in our sink, she burst into tears and said she couldn't stand this rotten dump a day longer. So maybe . . . maybe she had gone too.

The ceiling suddenly seemed a long long way off. I felt I was getting smaller and smaller until I wasn't much more than a squeak. I hunched up on the floor with my head on my knees and held on tight in case I disappeared altogether.

"Elsa? What on earth are you doing?" said Mum, coming down the corridor.

Yes, it was Mum, and I was *so* pleased to see her even though she sounded cross. And I was very pleased to see Pippa even though she was all sniffly with her nose running. And I was very pleased to see Hank even though he was howling his head off and needing his nappy changed. And I was . . . No. I wasn't very pleased to see Mack. I wouldn't ever go *that* far.

"Where have you *been?* I've been back from school for hours and hours!"

"Yeah, well, I'm sorry, love, but it's not our fault. We had a fight with that useless Manager this morning because we're all going to end up getting typhoid or cholera stuck in this dump, and the tight-fisted pig won't even send for a plumber to fix things, would you believe! Anyway, he said we could move out if we didn't like it here, and so I said we were doing our best to do just that, but we didn't have any place to go, so *then* we went down to the Housing Office, all of us, and would you believe they kept us waiting *all* day. They weren't even going to see us at all because we didn't have some stupid appointment, but we sat it out and I knew you'd be waiting, pet, but I couldn't do anything, could I?"

"So what happened, Mum? Are we getting a house?"

"The heck we are," said Mum. "They just mumbled on about priority families and exceptional circumstances and said even if this dump was affecting our health we'd have to get some really bad complaint and it would all have to be written up in medical reports and even then, if we were all at death's door, they couldn't guarantee us a house or even a moldy old apartment like we used to have."

"So I asked what *would* guarantee us a house—did one of you kids have to get sick and die? It just could happen," Mack said. "Look at little Pippa, all sniffles. She can't get rid of that cold, and as for the baby, well, I don't like the sound of his chest at all."

Mack sighed over Hank, who was still exercising his magnificent lungs. They certainly sounded in full working order.

"Yeah, Mack started to get really angry. Well, I did too, especially when they said they couldn't even guarantee us a set of rooms here like we're entitled to, instead of us being squashed like sardines. They said there was nothing further they could do at this moment in time, and they threatened to call the police unless we left the office."

Mum sighed theatrically, the back of her hand to her forehead. She might not be a real actress but it certainly sounded as if she'd been giving a good performance down at the Housing Office. She threatened to go back again tomorrow too.

"Yes, good thinking, Mum," I said, encouraging her so she wouldn't come to pick me up from school and crack my credibility.

Only I needn't have bothered. Someone else started telling the wrong sort of tales the very next day. Someone with a funny face. And a great big mouth.

Funny-Face got shoved in the special class too.

Right next to me, at the front, under the Fisher's pop eyes. This reminded me of 101 Popeye the Sailorman jokes—you know—and I swapped some of them with Funny-Face and we both got terrible snorty giggles, and Mrs. Fisher's eyes popped so much they almost rolled down her cheeks, and her mouth went so tight her lips disappeared.

"I'm glad you two are finding school so amusing," she said, very sarcastically. "Perhaps you'd like to share your little jokes with me, hmm?"

Perhaps not. If she heard some of the wilder Popeye jokes she'd explode.

So Funny-Face and I were getting along really well until playtime. And then one of the kids in the class asked if Funny-Face performed too.

"What?" said Funny-Face.

"Are you a child star like Elsarina and Pipette?" They started talking about the famous fictional talents of me and my family, and Funny-Face cracked up, thinking this was just another one of my jokes.

"You're all crazy," said Funny-Face. "How come you've fallen for all this rubbish? Elsa isn't a famous star! She's just a bed-and-breakfast kid, like me. And cripes, you should see her mum and her dopey little sister—they're not stars!"

That was enough. Funny-Face saw stars then. Because I punched him right in the nose.

All the children started shouting "Fight!

Fight! Fight!" I was all set to have a good fight even though I'm generally gentle, and Funny-Face was bewildered but wanted a fight too because I'd made his nose bleed. But as soon as we were ready to go Mrs. Fisher came flying forth and she seized Funny-Face in one hand and me in the other. She shook us both very vigorously indeed, practically clonking our heads together, and told us we were very rough, naughty children and we had to learn not to be violent in school.

Then, as she stalked off, she said just one word. Well, she muttered it, but I heard. And

Funny-Face did too. She said "*Typical.*" She meant we were typical bed-and-breakfast kids indulging in typical disruptive behavior. And I suddenly felt sick, as if I needed my bed and might well throw up my breakfast.

Funny-Face didn't look too clever either. He wiped the smear of blood from his nose and made a hideous face at Mrs. Fisher's back, crossing his eyes and waggling his tongue.

I giggled feebly.

"Why did the teacher have crossed eyes, eh? Because she couldn't control her pupils."

It was one of my least funny jokes but Funny-

Face guffawed politely.

"Well, she's not going to control us, is she, Elsa?"

"You bet she's not." His nose was still bleeding. I felt up my sleeve for a crumpled tissue. "Here," I said, dabbing at him.

"Stop it! You're acting like my mum," said Funny-Face.

"Sorry I socked you," I said.

"Yeah, well, if that old trout hadn't come along I'd have flattened you. Just as well for you. Though you can hit quite hard—for a girl."

"If you start that I'll hit you even harder," I said, but I gave his nose another careful wipe. "We're still mates, aren't we?"

"Course we are. But why did you have to attack me like that, eh?"

"Because of what you said about my mum and my sister."

"But you were the one telling porky-pies,* not me! Why did you spin all those stupid stories about them? I mean, it's crazy. As if you all could ever be in show biz."

"We could, you know," I said fiercely. "Well,

*porky-pies* Real pork pies are cold meat in pastry. Porky pies is slang for lies.

maybe not my mum. Or Pippa. But *I'm* going to be some day. I'll be famous, just you wait and see. I'll be a comedienne—that's a lady who tells jokes—and I'll have my own show and I'll get to be on the telly, you'll see, maybe sooner than you think."

It was sooner than I thought, too. Because when Funny-Face and I went home from school that day there was a camera crew filming in the lobby of the Royal Hotel!

# Chapter 9

"What on earth's going on?" said Funny-Face. "Hey, is this for telly? Are we going to be on the telly?"

He made a grotesque funny face for the camera, waving both his arms.

I sighed scornfully. I wasn't going to behave like some idiotic amateur. I checked out all the people and spotted the man in the tightest jeans and the leather jacket. He just had to be the director. I walked right up to him, smiling.

"Hello, I'm Elsa, I live here and I'm going to be a comedienne when I grow up. In fact, I've got my whole comedy act worked out right now. Would you like to listen?"

The director blinked rapidly behind his trendy glasses, but he seemed interested.

"You live here, do you, Elsa? Great, well, we're doing a program called 'Children in Crisis,' OK? Shall we do a little interview with you and your friend, eh? You can tell us all about how awful it is to have to stay in a bed-and-breakfast hotel, right?"

"Wrong, wrong, wrong!" said the bunny lady receptionist, rushing out from behind her desk. Even the telephone lady had put down her book and was peering out from behind her glass door.

141

"Go and get the Manager, quick," the bunny lady commanded, shooing the telephone lady up the hall. "Now listen to me, you television people. You're trespassing. Get out of this hotel right this minute or I'll call the police and have you evicted."

"I can tell any joke you like," I said to the director. "We'll have a police joke, OK? What did the policeman say to the three-headed man? 'Hello hello hello.' What's the police dog's telephone number? Canine Canine Canine."

"Very funny, dear," said the director, though he didn't laugh. "Now, once we get the camera rolling I want you to say a little about the crowded room you live in and how damp it is and maybe how there are nasty bugs in the bath, OK?"

"How dare you! This is a scrupulously clean establishment—there are no bugs here, no infestations of any kind!" the bunny lady screeched, so cross that the fluff on her sweater quivered.

"Bugs, OK, I'll tell you an insect joke, right? You've got this fly and this flea, yes, and when they fly past each other what time is it? Fly past flea." I laughed to show that this was the punchline.

"Mmm, well. Simmer down now, sweetie, we want you looking really sad for the camera. And you, sonny, do you think you could stop making those faces for five seconds?"

"OK, I can look sad, it's all part of a comedienne's repertoire. Look, is this sad enough?"

"Well, you needn't go to extremes. Cheer up just a bit."

"Hey, I've thought of another insect joke. There were these two little flies running like mad over a cornflake box—and do you know why? Because it said, 'Tear along dotted line.' "

I laughed, but that made me cheer up a bit too much. And then the Manager came charging up and started shouting and swearing at the television people and they tried to film him and he put his hand over the camera and I started to get the feeling I might have lost my big chance to make it on television.

"Phone the police this minute!" the Manager commanded.

"I know some more police jokes," I said, but no one was listening.

"Who put you up to this? Who invited you in, eh? Has one of the residents been complaining? Which one? You tell me. If they don't like it here they can get out," the Manager shouted, making wild gestures. He nearly clipped me on the head and I ducked. "It was your mum and dad, wasn't it, little girl!"

"That man's not my dad."

"The big Scottish fellow, he was throwing his weight around and moaning about his bathroom sink."

"What animal are you like when you take a bath? A little bear," I said, but I seemed to have lost my audience.

The police arrived and there was a big argument which ended in the camera crew having to squeeze all their stuff back around the revolving door, while the Manager continued to rant and rave at me, saying it was all my family's fault and we'd better start packing our bags right this minute.

I began to feel very much like a Child in Crisis. I whizzed out after the camera crew, desperate for one last chance to be on the telly.

"Hey, don't go, don't pack up!" I yelled, as I saw them heaving their gear into a van. "Look, couldn't we do an interview in front of the hotel?

I'll be very sad—I could even try to cry if you like. Look, I can make my face crumple up—or I tell you what, I'll go and get my little sister and brother from our room, they're great at crying—"

"Sorry, sweetie, but I think this is a waste of time," said the director. "I don't need this sort of hassle. And besides, you're a great little sport but you're not the sort of kid I'm looking for. I need someone . . . " He waved his hand in the air, unable to express exactly what he wanted. Then he stopped and stood still.

"Someone like that little kid there!" he said, snapping his fingers.

I looked for this lucky little kid. And do you know who it was? Naomi, mooching along the road, trailing a brother in either hand, looking all fed up and forlorn because I'd rushed off with Funny-Face instead of waiting for her.

"Hey, sweetie, over here!" The director waved at her frantically. "Where did you come from, hmm? Do you live in the bed-and-breakfast hotel by any chance?"

Naomi nodded nervously, clutching her little brothers.

"Great!" He threw back his head and addressed the clouds. "A gift!"

"We don't want any gifts. We don't take stuff from strangers," said Naomi, and she started trying to hustle her brothers away. She hustled a little too fast, and Neil tripped and started crying.

"Hey, shut up, little squirt," said Funny-Face. "You're going to be on the telly. Can I still be on it too, mister?"

"And me?" I said urgently.

"Well, you can maybe sort of wander in the background," said the director. "But no clowning. No funny faces. And absolutely *no* jokes."

I didn't actually feel like cracking any jokes right that minute. Naomi was going to be the star of the show. Not me, even though I'd been perfecting my routine and practicing on everyone all this time. Naomi, who couldn't crack a joke to save her life, little meek and mousey Naomi!

OK, I thought. Maybe just *one* joke to try to cheer myself up. So I whispered all to myself,

"What do you get if you cross an elephant with a mouse? Great big holes in the baseboard!" I couldn't help laughing. You can't really do that quietly. The director glared in my direction. "Dear goodness, you dippy kids! I don't want merriment, I don't want laughter, I don't want JOKES."

"OK, OK, no jokes," I said and I pinched my lips together with my fingers so he could see I was serious. Only it was such a pity. The mouse and elephant joke had triggered off a whole herd of elephant jokes inside my head, and they were trumpeting tremendously.

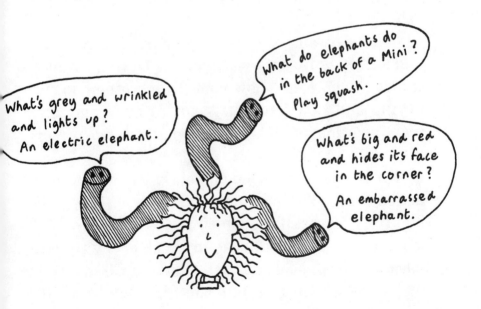

What's grey and wrinkled and lights up? An electric elephant.

What do elephants do in the back of a Mini? Play squash.

What's big and red and hides its face in the corner? An embarrassed elephant.

"Well *I* can't tell jokes," said Naomi truthfully. "I can't dance or sing or anything. So you'd really better pick Elsa."

"Oh Naomi," I said, immensely touched. "You can't do all the showy things, but you're really brainy. You could get to be on one of the quiz shows, eh?"

"Never mind quiz shows. This little girl's perfect for 'Children in Crisis.' Now just stand here, sweetie—little brothers too, that's it, and I'll ask you a few questions while the camera rolls, OK?"

"No, wait! Neil, come and get your nose wiped and stop that silly sniffling," Naomi said urgently. "And you, Nicky, pull your socks up."

"No, we want you just as you are, runny nose and all! Now I want you to tell me how miserable it is in the hotel and how your little brothers keep crying and how lousy it is not to have enough money for lots of dolls and video games like other kids. OK, action!"

Naomi chewed her lip anxiously, not going into action at all. She was thinking hard.

"It *is* miserable sometimes. But my mum gives me a cuddle or I read my book or my friend Elsa tells me a joke and then I cheer up."

I cheered up too, but the director seemed

148

determined to damp everything down. He practically told Naomi what she had to say.

The first time she tried she sounded all weird and wooden, and she kept looking up at the director anxiously and hissing, "Is that right? Have I remembered it?"

"No, sweetie, don't keep saying that. Just act natural, for pity's sake," said the director, practically tearing his hair.

The bunny lady receptionist came clopping out into the street in her high heels, wagging her pointed nails at the television crew.

"Now look! You're harassing our tenants. We'll call the police again. The Manager's on the phone right this minute. And as for you kids, I'm warning you. We don't have to house you, you know. If you've got any complaints then you can go somewhere else."

She clip-clopped back into the hotel. Naomi stared after her worriedly, her eyes filling with tears.

"Does she mean that? She wouldn't really throw us out, would she?" Naomi whispered. "We haven't got anywhere else to go. And it's so unfair, because we've put up with such a lot—we've even had those horrible bugs, cockroaches, squiggling all over the floor. One even got in the toe of our baby Nathan's bootee, and yet the Manager wouldn't even send for the pest-control people. He said it was our fault because we were dirty! And my mum cried when he said that because we're as clean as we can be— we bathe every day even when there isn't any hot water, and my mum keeps the room spotless, and that's not easy with the four of us kids. I don't know what we're going to do, because we've been waiting six months and we still can't get an apartment and if we get thrown out of the hotel then us kids will have to go into Foster Care and we've got to stay with our mum."

"We want our mum," said Nicky.

"Mum! Mum!" wailed Neil.

"Perfect!" said the director. The cameras had been rolling for all of Naomi's outburst. "Absolutely great, sweetie. Lovely emotive stuff. All right folks, I think we can hit the road now."

"But what about us?" said Naomi, wiping her eyes. "Are we going to get thrown out?"

"Mmm? Oh, I shouldn't think so," he said vaguely.

He'd turned his back on us. He didn't know. He didn't even care. He just wanted to make a good television program.

I put my arm round Naomi. "We'll be OK," I said, giving her a hug. "Don't take any notice of him. He's just been using us. Still, it looks like you really will be on the telly after all, Naomi."

Naomi didn't seem very thrilled about the idea. She still worried and worried that her family might get thrown out.

"Look, they've threatened us too. That Manager thinks it's all my mum and Mack's fault. We'll all be thrown out together. We'll have to set up a little camp. It's OK, Naomi. Don't get so upset."

I tried to cheer her up, but it wasn't easy.

"I wish you hadn't got us all involved with those telly people," Naomi said, sighing.

That's what Mum and Mack were saying too in room 608. Only they were saying it a lot more angrily. I could hear them yelling from right down the corridor.

"Oh-oh," I said.

"It's all your fault, you big Scottish dope!" Mum was screaming. "You shouldn't have phoned them. Now that Manager will make our lives a misery."

"It's a flaming misery as it is. It couldn't be worse. I was simply trying to help, so stop giving me all this hassle, woman."

I slunk into the room. Pippa was crouched in the duck crib, clutching Baby Pillow. Hank was whimpering in bed, needing his nappy changed. I mopped them up and crept off with them. I don't think Mum and Mack even noticed.

It was getting near teatime and there were lots of cooking smells coming from the kitchen. Mum still said it was a filthy hole and we couldn't cook in there or we'd get a terrible disease. I was starting to get so starving hungry I was willing to risk the terrible disease, but we didn't have anything to cook.

Naomi's mum was stirring a very interesting bean stew that smelled ever so rich and tasty. She had baby Nathan on her hip, and he was smacking his lips in happy anticipation.

Naomi told her mum all about the television people and the Manager's threats, but Naomi's mum didn't get mad at all. She just went on stirring her stew.

"We'll be fine, little old lady," she said to Naomi. "You're such a worry-guts. Here, tea's just about ready. Have you got the plates set out in our room?"

She saw Pippa and Hank and me looking at her hungrily.

"Do you kids want to come and join us for tea?" she said cheerily.

We wanted to extremely badly, but there wasn't that much stew and it seemed a bit selfish to eat their food so I said we'd be having our own tea in a minute.

But when we went back to room 608 the fight was getting louder and fiercer and I knew there was no point disturbing them. So Pippa and Hank and I hung around the kitchen some more. Simple Simon's mum came along and she cooked a whole load of chips in the greasy old chip-pan—so many that they almost came bubbling over the top. They smelled so good and she had such a lot that I decided we'd have a few if she offered. Only she didn't.

Simon's mum was very fierce.

"What are you kids staring at?" she said sharply. "Clear out of here. Go and get your own tea."

But that was easier said than done. The fight was still roaring. So we sat outside the room, our tummies rumbling. Mack came storming out eventually. He tripped right over me actually. I felt like calling him a big Scottish dope too, but I sensed it wasn't quite the moment. I knew where he was going. Down to the pub. And he wouldn't be back for ages.

At least that meant we could get in our room. But Mum didn't seem up to thinking about something ordinary like tea. She was in bed crying and when I tried to talk to her she pulled the covers up over her head. She went on crying for a bit and then she went to sleep.

I felt really funny for about five minutes. Not funny ha-ha. Funny peculiar and horrible. It hadn't been a good day. I wasn't going to be on television. I didn't have any tea. I felt like getting into my own bed and pulling the covers up and having a good cry.

But Pippa and Hank were looking up at me and I couldn't let them down. I switched on the telly and said they could stay up as long as they liked because Mum was asleep and Mack was out.

And I hunted around the room for food and found some stale sliced bread and a jar of raspberry jam.

"We're going to have a really special tea, you'll see," I said, searching through Mum's handbag for her nail scissors. I got snipping and cutting and made us ultra-special jam sandwiches.

I made a clown jam sandwich for Hank.

I made a teddy jam sandwich for Pippa and Baby Pillow.

And I made a great red movie-star-lip sandwich for me, and the jammy lips kissed me for being such a good girl.

## Chapter 10

I woke up early and read my joke books in bed . . .

Why are tall people lazier than short people? Because they're longer in bed, ha ha!

. . . and then Pippa woke up for a cuddle and Hank woke up for a bottle and soon it was time to get up.

Mum didn't wake up. Mack didn't wake up either. He was snoring like a warthog with a cold.

So I had to speak up to make myself heard.

Mum stirred at last.

"Will you stop that shouting, Elsa!"

"I'm *not* shouting," I said, wounded. "I'm simply speaking up a little because that Scottish dope is snoring fit to bust."

Mum stirred more vigorously.

"Don't you dare call Mack names like that, you cheeky little whatsit!"

"But that's what *you* called him just last night."

We started to have a little argument. I might have gotten a bit heated. Suddenly the warthog stopped snoring. It reared up in the bed, a horrible sight.

"If you don't stop that shouting and screaming right this minute, Elsa, I'll give you such a smacking you'll never dare say another word."

He glared at me with his bleary eyes and then slowly subsided back under the covers. Hank gave a worried hiccup. Pippa started sucking her fingers. I blinked hard at the bulk in the bed. I opened my mouth, but Pippa shook her head and clutched me with her dribbly little hands. I gave her a hug to show her it was OK. I wasn't going to speak. Mack might be an idle jerk but he doesn't make idle threats. He always follows them through.

I waggled my tongue very impressively at the bed instead. Mum still had her eyes open and she didn't tell me off. When I went to take Pippa and Hank downstairs for breakfast she sat up in bed and held her arms out to me.

"I'm sorry, love," she whispered. "I didn't mean to get you into trouble. You're a good girl really, I know you are. I don't know what I'd do without you."

I cheered up a bit then, but when we went down to breakfast the bunny lady said loudly to the telephone lady: "Oh-oh, there's one of the little troublemakers." She pointed at me with a lilac fingernail to match a new purple fluffy

sweater. "The Manager wants to see your dad in his office," she announced.

"He's not my dad," I said and walked straight past, Hank on my hip, Pippa hanging on my hand.

"Mack is my dad," Pippa whispered. "Is he going to get into trouble, Elsa?"

"I don't know," I said uncomfortably. Maybe we were all in trouble. Maybe we really were going to get thrown out.

We went to sit with Naomi and her family at breakfast. They were looking dead gloomy too. Naomi's mum didn't smile at me the way she usually did.

"I'll tell you a really good joke about cornflakes," I said.

"No jokes, Elsa," she said, sighing.

"OK, I'll tell you this cornflake joke tomorrow. It's a cereal," I said. I roared with laughter. It wasn't *that* funny, but I wanted to lighten the atmosphere.

Naomi's mum stayed gloomy. Naomi chewed her lip anxiously. Even Nicky and Neil couldn't crack a smile.

"What's up, eh?" I said, starting to feed baby Nathan, playing the airplane game.

He at least seemed happy enough to play but Naomi's mum caught hold of my arm and took away my spoon.

"No, leave him be. Leave all my family be. Haven't you done enough?"

"Oh, Mum," said Naomi. "It isn't Elsa's fault."

"She was the one who talked you into that television interview," said Naomi's mum. "And now the Manager says we'll have to go."

"Well, he says we've got to go too. But he doesn't mean it. He just wants to scare us," I said. I tried to sound reassuring but I was getting scared too. "Look, I'll go and see the Manager. I'll tell him it was all my fault if you like. Then at least you'll be OK."

So after we'd had breakfast I lumped Hank along to the Manager's office, Pippa trailing behind us. I didn't have a hand free to knock so we just went barging straight into his office. The Manager wasn't alone. He wasn't having a little

160

cuddle with the bunny lady. He was with Mrs.
Hoover, and he didn't look at all cuddly. He was
telling Mrs. Hoover off, wagging his finger at her.

"What's the matter?" I said. "Why is he being
nasty to you, Mrs. Hoover?

"You! Out of my office this instant," said the
Manager. "It's your mum and dad I want to see,
not *you*."

"I keep telling you, I haven't *got* a dad. That
Scottish guy is nothing to do with me," I insisted.

"Oh yes! Thank you for reminding me. Yes,
my receptionist informs me that there's more disgusting graffiti about a Scots person inside the
ladies' downstairs bathroom," said the Manager,
still wag-wag-wagging that finger at poor Mrs.
Hoover.

"She didn't do that! I know for a fact that Mrs. Hoover didn't write all that stuff on the walls," I said quickly, my heart thumping. Everyone seemed to be getting into trouble because of me and it was awful. I decided to make a clean breast of things. (What a weird expression. I haven't even got a breast yet. And even if I did it wouldn't be clean because the sink in room 608 was getting so grungy I haven't felt very much like washing recently.)

"All the Mack jokes—they're mine," I said.

The Manager and Mrs. Hoover both blinked at me.

"You wrote all that revolting rubbish?" said the Manager.

"I thought some of the jokes were quite funny," I mumbled.

"You children! Vandals! Hooligans!" said the Manager.

"It was just me. Not Pippa. She can't write yet—and even if she could, she quite likes her dad. It's just me that can't stand him. So you can stop telling Mrs. Hoover off because, like I said, it was me."

"Oh Elsa," said Mrs. Hoover. "He knows I didn't write it, silly. He's cross because I can't clean it all off. I keep telling him that felt-tip just won't budge even though I scrub and scrub."

"I never see you scrubbing. The hotel is a disgrace. No wonder we have television crews traipsing in here making trouble. If I'm reported to the authorities it will be all your fault."

"If you get reported to the authorities it'll be because you run a lousy hotel," said Mrs. Hoover. "How can I possibly hope to keep up a huge place like this? Why don't you employ more staff?"

"I'll be employing one less member of staff if you don't watch your tongue," said the Manager.

"All right then. That suits me. You can take your stupid job," said Mrs. Hoover whipping off her smock and throwing it right in his face.

Then she turned on her heel and flounced straight out of his office. I decided it wasn't quite the right time to plead Naomi's case to the Manager. I ran after Mrs. Hoover instead.

"Oh gosh, have you really lost your job now? And it's my fault because I did all the scribbling on the walls," I wailed. "Oh Mrs. Hoover, I'm so sorry!"

"Mrs. Whoosit?" said Mrs. Hoover. "Here, is that what you kids call me? Well, don't you fret yourself, pet. I've had it up to here vacuuming for that dreadful man. I'll get another cleaning job—they're not that hard to come by even nowadays."

But I couldn't be absolutely sure she was telling the truth. I wished I was as little as Pippa so she could pick me up and give me a big hug to reassure me. I felt little inside. And stupid. And sad. And sorry.

I was extra loud and noisy and bouncy and bossy at school to try to make myself feel big again. It didn't work. I kept telling jokes to Funny-Face and he kept laughing, but Mrs. Fisher was frowning and she made us stay in at playtime and write out I MUST LEARN TO BEHAVE PROPERLY IN THE CLASSROOM fifty times.

Funny-Face is not very good at writing. His words wobble up over the line and slide down below it. His spelling's a bit wobbly too. He left out one *s* in *classroom*. Mrs. Fisher pointed this out huffily. I was scared she might make him do it all over again, so I tried to lighten things a little.

"Why can't you remember there are two *s*'s in

*class*?" she said crossly. "I've told you enough times."

"Which *s* did he leave out this time, Mrs. Fisher?" I said.

It was a joke. A bit of a feeble one, but a joke all the same. Only Mrs. Fisher just thought I was being cheeky.

Do you know what happened? We had to stay in at lunchtime too. Funny-Face had to write out CLASSROOM another fifty times, and I had to write out a fresh fifty: I MUST LEARN NOT TO BE CHEEKY IN THE CLASSROOM.

"That's silly, anyway," I muttered. "That sounds like I can be cheeky in the hall and cheeky in the corridors and cheeky in the toilets and cheeky all over the place. And I wasn't blooming cheeky to start with. I was just joking."

"You and your *@!+!@* jokes!" said Funny-Face, laboriously drawing *s*'s.

"Hey, don't be like that. Listen, this boy was kept in at lunchtime just like us and his teacher said he had to write out this sentence of less than fifty words, right? So do you know what he wrote?"

"No, and I don't care," said Funny-Face. "Here, I've got all these stupid *s*'s in the right place, haven't I?"

"Yes. Though hang on, you've started to miss out your *o*'s now. There are two in *classroom*. Like us two in this classroom. But listen to the punchline of my joke. This boy wrote, "I went to call my cat in for the night so I stood at the door and called: 'Here, kitty, kitty, kitty, kitty, kitty...'"

"Shut *up*, Elsa."

"No, I haven't done enough kittys—there are supposed to be fifty. And you've missed out another *o* there—*and* there."

"You'll be going O in a minute, when I punch you right in the nose," Funny-Face growled.

"What do you give a pig with a sore nose? Oinkment," I said, snorting like a little pig myself because I think that's one of my funnier jokes.

"Why don't you shut your cakehole?" he said, and he sounded so menacing I did what he said.

I wished he hadn't used that expression. We

still hadn't been allowed to have our lunch and I kept thinking very wistfully of cake. When horrible old Mrs. Fisher eventually let us go, we had to squeeze in right at the end of second-sitting lunch, when all the goodies had long since gone. Not one chip left. We had to make do with a salad, and no one ever chooses bunny food from choice. I know some excellent bunny jokes but I decided it might be better to keep them in their burrow in my head. Funny-Face still didn't look ready for mirth as he chomped his way morosely through his lettuce.

We had a new teacher in the hall in the afternoon to take us for singing. It was a relief to be free of the Fishy-Eye and I was all set to sing my cares away. I didn't know many of the songs but I've always been good at improvising. So I threw back my head and let it rip. But the teacher stopped playing the piano. Her face was all screwed up as if she had a terrible headache.

"Who is making that . . . noise?" she asked.

We stared at her. What did she mean? We were all making noise. We were singing.

Only she didn't seem to appreciate that. She made us start again, this time without the piano. I decided not to let this faze me. I sang out joyfully. The teacher shuddered.

"You!" she said, pointing.

I peered round. No, it wasn't anyone else. She was pointing at me.

"Yes, you. The little bed-and-breakfast girl."

The other children around me snickered. I felt my face start to burn, like the Royal Hotel's toast.

"Could you try not to sing so loudly, please?" said the teacher.

"Why?" I asked, astonished.

"Because you're singing rather flat, dear. And completely out of tune. In fact, it might be better if you didn't sing at all, even softly. How about just nodding your head in time to the music?"

The other kids collapsed, nudging each other and tittering.

"Some stage star, eh? She can't even sing in tune," they hissed.

I had to spend the whole singing lesson with my mouth shut, nid-nodding away. I didn't feel much like making a noise after that. I hardly said anything on the way home from school.

"What's up, Elsa?" said Naomi, putting her arm round me. "Here, I'm sorry my mum got mad at you. It wasn't really fair for her to pick on you."

"Oh, I don't know. That's what everyone does. Pick on me," I said gloomily.

"Hey, don't be like that. You're always so cheerful. I can't bear it when you're all sad. Tell us a joke, go on."

But for the first time in my life I didn't even

feel like telling jokes. Mum gave me a big hug when I went up to room 608. She sent Mack out for a special Kentucky chicken tea.

"To make up for last night, lovie," said Mum. "Sorry about that. And Mack's sorry he got snappy too. He's feeling better now."

Mack might be feeling better, Mum might be feeling better. I didn't feel better at all.

I normally love Kentucky chicken takeaways. I like to sit cross-legged on the floor with Pippa and pretend we're American pioneers like in *Little House on the Prairie,* and we're eating a chicken our Pa has raised and there are prowling bears outside who can smell it cooking but we're safe inside our little log cabin.

"Play our game," Pippa commanded, but somehow I couldn't make it work.

I usually finish off the game by pretending Hank is a baby bear cub and we all feed him bits of chicken (Hank loves this game too) and then we have a jolly sing-song. But now I didn't feel I ever wanted to sing again.

I didn't want to say anything.
I didn't want to tell jokes.
I didn't want to be me.

"Do try and cheer up, Elsa," said Mum. "Come on, you're going to have to go to bed if you sulk around the room like this."

"I don't care," I said.

So I went to bed really early, before Pippa— even before Hank. Of course it was difficult to get to sleep when the light was on and the telly was loud and there were two and a half people and a baby still racketing around the room, but I put my head way down under the covers and curled up in a little ball with my hands over my ears.

When I woke up I couldn't hear anything even when I took my hands away. I stuck my head out the covers. I could hardly see anything either in the dark. It seemed like the middle of the night.

And yet . . . someone was cooking supper somewhere. I could smell chips. People sometimes stayed up really late and made midnight snacks. I licked my lips. I hadn't eaten all my Kentucky chicken because I'd felt so fed up. I could do with a little snack now myself.

I wondered who was cooking in the kitchen. I'd got to know most of our sixth floor by now. Most of them were quite matey with me. I wondered if they'd consider sharing a chip or two.

I eased myself out of bed. Pippa mumbled

something in her sleep, but didn't wake up. I picked my way across the crowded floor, tripping over Pippa's My Little Pony and stepping straight into a Kentucky chicken carton, but eventually I reached the door. I opened it very slowly so that it wouldn't make any noise and crept outside into the corridor. Then I stood still, puzzled. There was a much stronger smell now. And there was a strange flickering light coming from right down the end, in the kitchen. And smoke. You don't get smoke without . . . FIRE!

# Chapter 11

## We Nearly Have Our Chips!

For just one second I stood still, staring. And then I threw back my head and gave a great lion roar.

"FIRE!" I shouted. "FIRE FIRE FIRE!"

I banged on room 612, I banged on room 611, I banged on room 610, I banged on room 609, charging wildly back down the corridor and bellowing all the while.

"FIRE FIRE FIRE FIRE FIRE FIRE !"

I shouted so long and so loud it felt as if there was a fire in my own head, red and roaring. And then I got to room 608 and I went hurtling inside, screaming and shouting as I snapped on the light.

"FIRE!" I flew to Mum and shook her shoulder hard. Mack propped himself up on one elbow, his eyes bleary. "Shut that racket!" he mumbled.

"I can't! There's a fire in the kitchen. Oh, quick, quick, Mum, wake up! Pippa, get up, come on, out of bed."

Mum sat up, shaking her head, still half-asleep. It was Mack who suddenly shot straight out, grabbing Hank from one bed, Pippa from the other.

"It's OK, Elsa, I'll get them out. You wake the others along the corridor," he said, busy and brisk.

"Oh good lord, what are we going to do?" Mum said, stumbling out of bed, frantic. "Quick kids, get dressed as soon as you can—I'll do Hank."

"No, no, there's no time. We've just got to get out," said Mack. "No clothes, no toys, no messing about—OUT!"

"Baby Pillow!" Pippa yelled, struggling, but

Mack held her tight.

"I've got him," I said, snatching Baby Pillow from Pippa's bed.

Then I went charging down the corridor, calling, "FIRE FIRE FIRE!" all over again.

The smoke was stronger now, and I could hear this awful crackling sound down the corridor. One of the men went running towards the kitchen in his pajamas, but when he got near he slowed down and then backed away.

"Get everyone out!" he shouted. "The whole kitchen's ablaze. Keep yelling, little kid. Wake them all up, loud as you can."

I took a huge breath and roared the dreadful warning over and over again. Some people came running out right away. Others shouted back, and someone started screaming that we were all going to be burned alive.

"No one will be burned alive if you all just stop panicking," Mack shouted, charging down the corridor, Pippa under one arm, Hank under the other, Mum stumbling along in her nightie behind them. Mack was only wearing his underwear and any other time in the world I'd have rolled around laughing, he looked such a sight.

But we all looked sights. People came blundering out of their bedrooms in nighties and

pajamas and T-shirts and underwear. Some were clutching handbags, some had suitcases, several had shoved their possessions in blankets and were dragging them along the hall.

"Leave all your bits and bobs behind. Let's just get out down the stairs. Carry the kids. Come on, get cracking!" Mack yelled. He banged his fist against the fire alarm at the end of the corridor and it started ringing.

"You race down to the fifth floor and get that alarm going too, Elsa!" Mack yelled. "And keep calling 'Fire!' Go on, pal, you're doing great."

I shot off down the stairs and searched for the fifth-floor fire alarm—but it had already been broken weeks ago by some of the boys and no one had ever got around to mending it. But *I* wasn't broken. I was in full working order.

"FIRE!" I roared. "Get up, get out! Come on, wake up! FIRE FIRE FIRE!"

I ran the length of the corridor and back, banging on every door, screeching until my throat was sore. Then I rushed down the stairs, pushing past sleepy people stumbling in their nightclothes, desperate to find Mum and Pippa and Hank and Mack, wanting to make sure they were safe.

"Elsa! Elsa, where are you? Come here, baby!"

It was Mum, forcing her way back up to the fifth floor, shouting and screaming.

"Oh Elsa!" she cried, and she swooped on me, clutching me as if she could never let me go. "I thought you were with us—and then I looked back and you weren't there and I had to come back to get you even though Mack kept telling me you were fine and you were just waking everyone up . . . Oh Elsa, lovie, you're safe!"

"Of course I'm safe, Mum," I said, hugging her fiercely. "But I've got to get cracking down on the fourth floor now. No one else has got such a good voice as me. Listen. FIRE!"

I nearly knocked Mum over with the force of my voice.

"Goodness! Yes, well, I don't see how anyone can sleep through that. But it's OK, they've got the other fire alarms going now and some of the men are seeing that everyone's getting out. They've rung for the fire engines. So come on now, darling—hang on tight to my hand," said Mum.

We made our way down the stairs, clinging to each other. There was no smoke on the lower floors but people were still panicking, surging out and running like mad, pushing and shoving. One little kid fell down but his mum pulled him up again and one of the men popped him up on his shoulders out of harm's way. The stairs seemed to go on forever, as if we were going down and down right into the middle of the earth, but at last the linoleum changed to the carpeting and then even though our feet kept trying to run downwards, we were on the ground floor.

The Manager was there in a fancy camel dressing gown, wringing his hands.

"Which one of you crazies set my hotel on fire?" he screamed. "I'll have the law on you!"

"And we'll have the law on you too, because your fire alarms aren't working properly and we could all have got roasted to a cinder if it wasn't for my kid," Mack thundered. He was still clutching Pippa in one arm, Hank in another. He turned to me—and for one mad moment I thought he was going to try to pick me up too. "Yeah, this little kid here! She raised the alarm. She got us all up and out of it. Our Elsa."

I'm not Mack's Elsa and I never will be—but I didn't really mind him showing off about me all the same.

"That Elsa!"

"Yes, little Elsa—she yelled 'Fire!' fit to bust."

"She was the one who woke us up—that little kid with the loud voice."

They were all talking about me as we surged outside the hotel on to the pavement. Lots of people came and patted me on the back and said I'd done a grand job, and one man saw I was shivering out in the cold street and wrapped his sweater right around me to keep me warm. Someone had dragged out a whole pile of blankets

and the old ladies and little kids got first pick.
There weren't enough to go round.

"Come on, Jimmy, you can be a gent too," said
Mack, seizing hold of the Manager and "helping"
him out of his cozy camel dressing gown. He
draped it round a shivery Asian granny who nodded and smiled. The Manager was shaking his
head and frowning, ferociously. He looked even
sillier than Mack now, dressed in a pair of silky
boxer shorts and nothing else. The bunny receptionist looked a bit bedraggled too without her
angora sweater and with her fluffy hair in curlers.
Telephone looked startling in red satin pajamas—
a bit like a large raspberry jelly. Now that everyone was safe out in the street this fire was almost
starting to be fun.

Then we heard a distant clanging and a big cheer went up. The fire engines were coming! We all crowded out of their way, and firefighters in yellow helmets went rushing into the hotel with all their firefighting equipment. Lots of the kids wanted to go rushing in after them to watch. Funny-Face had to be hauled away by his mum, and Simple Simon and Nicky and Neil started their own fire-engine imitations, barging around bumping into people Even baby Hank got the idea and started shrieking like a siren.

Several ambulances arrived although no one had actually been hurt, and the police came too. And guess who else? A television crew. Not the "Children in Crisis" people. These were from one of the news stations. And there were reporters too, running around with notebooks, and photographers flashing away with their cameras although all the people in their underwear started shrieking. Everyone asked how the fire started and who discovered it and someone said "Elsa" and then someone else echoed them and soon almost everyone was saying "Elsa Elsa Elsa."

Me!

People were prodding me, pushing me forwards towards the cameras and the microphones and the notebooks. It was my Moment of Glory.

And do you know what? I can hardly bear to admit it. I got real shy. I just wanted to duck my head and hide behind my mum.

"Come on now, lovie. Tell us all about it. You were the one who raised the alarm, weren't you? Come on, sweetheart, no need to be shy. It sounds as if you've been very brave," they said. "Tell us in your own words exactly what happened."

I opened my mouth. But no words came out. It was as if I'd used up all my famous voice yelling "Fire!" so many times.

So someone else started speaking for me. The wrong someone. The someone who really doesn't have anything to do with me. We're not even related. Though now he was acting as if he was my dad and I was his daughter.

"The poor wee girl's still a bit stunned—and no wonder! My, but she did a grand job raising the alarm," Mack boasted, strutting all around. He was careful to hold in his tummy all the time the

cameras were pointing his way. He couldn't flex his arm muscles properly because he was still carrying Pippa and Hank, but he kept carefully arranging his legs as if he was posing for Mister Universe. He looked pretty silly. He sounded silly too, prattling on and on about his wee Elsa. If I'd had any voice left at all I'd have contradicted him furiously.

Then little Pippa piped up.

"Yes, my sister Elsa's ever so big and brave. She rescued my baby!"

"She rescued the baby?" said the reporters, looking at Hank.

"Yep, she went and got him out of his crib. I was crying and crying because I thought he'd get all burned up and Dad and Mum wouldn't let me go back for him—"

"They wouldn't go back for the *baby*?" said the reporters, their eyes swivelling from Hank to Mum and Mack.

"Not *our* baby. It's just Pippa's pillow. She calls it her baby," said Mum quickly. Then she realized the cameras were aiming at her, and she clutched her nightie with one hand and did her best to tidy her hair with the other. "Don't worry, we made sure we had our baby Hank safe and sound. But certainly if it hadn't been for our Elsa then we could still be in our beds right this minute—charred to cinders," said Mum dramatically.

"Yes, Elsa banged on our door and woke us all up. We'd be dead if it wasn't for her. She rescued all of us," said Naomi's mum. "Me and all *my* babies," she said showing them off to the camera.

"Elsa's my best friend," said Naomi, nodding her head so that her braids jiggled.

"Elsa's *my* best friend too and she rescued us and everyone," said Funny-Face, and then he made the funniest face he could manage, all cross-eyes and drooly mouth until his mum gave him a poke.

My mum was giving me a poke too.

"Come on then, pet. Haven't you got anything to say for yourself? All these nice gentlemen want you to say a few words about the fire. Come on, lovie, this is your big chance," Mum hissed.

I knew it. I swallowed. I wet my lips. I took a deep breath.

"Fire," I mumbled. It was as if my voice could still only say one thing. I concentrated fiercely, trying to gain control. Fire crackled through my thoughts. My brain suddenly glowed.

"Do you know what happened to the plastic surgeon who got too close to the fire?" I said, in almost my own voice.

"What plastic surgeon? There was a doctor in there? Did he get out OK?" the reporters clamored.

"He melted!" I said, and burst out laughing.

They blinked at me, missing a beat.

I decided to forge right ahead like a true professional.

"Who invented fire? Some bright spark!" I said, brightly and sparkily. Mum gave me a violent nudge.

"Elsa, stop telling those silly *jokes!*"

But once I got started I couldn't ever seem to stop.

"Why did the fireman wear red trousers?" I paused for a fraction. Everyone was still staring at me oddly. "His blue ones were at the cleaners!"

"Pack it in, Elsa," Mack hissed, looking like he wasn't so sure he wanted me to be his wee Elsa after all.

"It's the shock," said Mum firmly. "She's just having a funny five minutes."

"Only she's not being very funny," said Mack.

"Yep, I think we'd better cut the jokes," said the television man gently.

"I'll try harder," I said desperately. "I'll try a new set of jokes, OK? Or I could put on a silly voice . . . ?"

"Why not use your own voice, Elsa? And why do you have to try so hard? Just be yourself. Act natural," said the television man, chucking me under the chin. "Let's start again, hmm? Tell us in your own words exactly what happened."

"But if I just say any old thing, without any jokes, then I'm not funny," I wailed.

"Who says you've got to be funny?"

"Well, I want to be a comedienne and get to be famous."

"You don't have to be funny to be famous. And we don't really want people laughing when this goes out on the news. We want to touch the heart. We've got a super story here. You're a great little kid, Elsa. You'll come over really well on television if you just *relax*."

"It's kind of difficult to act relaxed when you're standing on the pavement in your T-shirt and knickers and a whole bunch of strangers are asking you questions," I said, sighing.

I wasn't trying to be funny. But the weirdest thing happened. Everyone chuckled appreciatively.

"So what happened, Elsa? You woke up in the middle of the night and . . . ?"

And so I started to tell them exactly what

happened. I said I thought the smell was someone cooking chips and I started to get hungry and
slipped out of bed to go and beg a few chips for
myself. (They laughed again.) Then I told about
tripping over Pippa's My Little Pony. (More
laughter—and I still hadn't told a single joke!)
Then I went on about the fire and dashing up and
down the corridor banging on the doors and
yelling. (I waited for them to laugh again, but
this time they listened spellbound.) The television man asked what I'd yelled and I said "Fire"
and he said that wasn't very loud and *I* said well,
I did it a lot louder. And he said show us. So I
did. I threw back my head and roared.

"F-I-I-I-I-I-I-I-I-I-I-I-I-I-I-I-I-I-I-I-R-E!!!"

That nearly blew them all backwards. Most
people had their hands over their ears. Some
shook their heads, dazed.
Then someone laughed.
They all joined in. Someone
else cheered.

Someone else did too.
Lots of cheers. For me.
FOR ME!

It really was my
Moment of Fame. I hadn't
blown it after all.

My interview went out on the television. I thought I sounded sort of stupid, but everyone else said it went splendidly. (Well, Mum moaned because her hair was a sight and she didn't have any make-up on, and Mack fussed because they'd cut out most of his parts and he was only shown from the waist up so no one could see his great hairy legs.) But they didn't cut *any* of my parts.

I might not have made it into the "Children in Crisis" documentary. But guess what. My news interview was repeated later in the year in a special program called "Children of Courage." And I got to do another interview with a nice blonde lady with big teeth, and Mum spent some of Mack's betting money on a beautiful new outfit from the Flowerfields Shopping Center for my special telly appearance.

Mum made me try on lots of frilly dresses but they all looked *awful*. So she gave up and let me choose instead. I wanted black jeans (so they wouldn't show the dirt). Mum bought me a black top too, and tied her red scarf round my neck, and then guess what we found at a sale? Red cowboy boots! They were a bit big but we stuffed the toes with paper and I looked absolutely great.

The blonde lady with the big teeth loved my outfit too. She said I looked just like a cowboy. I was a bit nervous so without thinking I got started on a cowboy joke routine.

"Who wears a cowboy hat and spurs and lives under the sea? Billy the Squid!"

She laughed! It wasn't *that* funny, one of my oldest jokes actually, but she laughed and laughed and laughed. She said she loved jokes, the older and cornier the better, and she said I could maybe come on her special show one day and do my own comedy routine!!!!!

# Chapter 12

## My Best and Biggest Ever Breakfast

We couldn't go back to bed in room 608 when the firemen put the fire out at last. It wasn't all burned to bits. It was only the kitchen that had cooked itself into little black crumbs. But the whole corridor was thick with smoke and sloshy with water and all the rooms looked as if someone had run around with giant paint-brushes and vats of black paint. All our stuff was covered in this black sticky stuff, and there was a sharp smell that scratched at your nostrils.

"Sorry, folks. You'll have to stay in temporary accommodations for a few weeks," said the Chief Fireman, shaking his head.

He looked surprised when all the residents of the Royal gave a hearty cheer. The Manager was prancing about in his silk boxer shorts, pointing out that only a few of the rooms were seriously fire-damaged and that the first few floors were barely affected. There was a lot of rushing around consulting and eventually it was decided that only the people living on the top two floors need be evacuated.

Us sixth-floor and fifth-floor people hugged and danced and shouted. All the other residents booed and argued and complained. Naomi and I had a big hug because she's on the fifth floor so she could come too. Then Funny-Face came and clapped hands with me because though he's on the fourth floor their room is right below the burned kitchen and water had swirled right down through the room underneath and was dripping through to them, so they couldn't stay either.

We were all carried off in police cars and buses to this church hall, where several big bossy ladies with cardigans over their nighties handed out blankets and pillows and sleeping bags. They gave us paper cups of hot soup too—which we needed, because the church hall was freezing. The floor was slippery linoleum and fun to skid across in your socks, but not exactly cozy or comfy when we settled down to go to sleep. I didn't exactly like Bed Number Eight—and it soon got crowded because Pippa unzipped my sleeping bag and

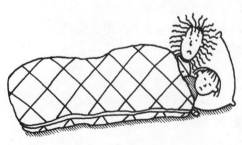

stuck herself in too. She kept having nightmares and twitching and I had to keep waking her up and dragging her off to the toilet because I was all too aware of what would happen if I didn't.

There was only one toilet and there were queues for it all night long. It was worse in the morning. There was only the one small wash basin too, and most people didn't have their toothbrushes or washcloths or towels anyway.

"I don't know why we were cheering last night," said Mum, trying to wipe round Hank's sticky face with a damp hankie. "Compared with this drafty old dump the Royal is practically a palace."

"We can't stay here," said Mack, sitting up and scratching. "I'm going right down that Housing Department first thing."

"Oh yeah?" said Mum, looking at him. "You're walking down the road in your underpants, right? Don't forget you haven't even got any trousers anymore. And look at me! This is all I've got—the old nightie that I'm wearing. All my clothes, all my make-up, my china-lady . . . all gone! Even if they're not ruined by that smoke then someone will have bound to steal them before I can get back to claim them." She started to cry so I went and put my arms round her.

"Don't cry, Mum," I said, hugging her tight. "You've still got us."

Mum snuffled a bit but then hugged me back.

"Yes, that's right, Elsa. I've still got my family. My Mack. My baby. My little girl. And my special big girl."

The special big girl got a bit snuffly herself then. I was glad that Funny-Face in the next row of sleeping bags was still fast asleep or he might have jeered. He looked oddly little, snuggled up under the blanket. And he sucked his thumb and all!

More big bossy ladies breezed into the hall and started heating up a big urn of tea. They had lots of packets of biscuits too. I helped hand them around to everyone. We could have seconds and even thirds. A custard cream, a shortbread finger and a chocolate Hob Nob make quite a good breakfast.

Then the ladies started dragging in great black plastic sacks crammed with clothes.

"Come and help yourselves! There should be enough for a new outfit for everyone."

"Oh, big deal," Mum grumbled. "It's just tatty old junk left over from garage sales. I'm not wearing anyone's old castoffs."

She watched Funny-Face's mum trying to

squeeze herself into a tight black skirt.

"She's wasting her time. She'll never get that over her big bum," Mum mumbled, and when Funny-Face's mum had to give up the attempt, Mum darted out and snatched the skirt herself.

"There! I thought so! That's a Betty Barclay skirt. I've seen them on sale in Flowerfields. Hey, look, does it fit?" Mum pulled it up over her narrow hips and stood admiring herself. "I wonder if there's a jacket to go with it, eh?"

Mum started skimming her way through the plastic sacks and came up with all sorts of goodies—even a pair of patent high heels her exact size. She had more trouble finding stuff for Mack, considering the only size he takes is *out*-size. She found a sweater that could just about go around him, but the biggest trousers could barely fit and the legs ended way above his ankles. Hank was a bit of a problem too—there were heaps of baby clothes, but he's such a *big* baby that the average one-year-old's sleeping suit came unpopped every time he breathed out and bent him up double into the bargain. Pippa was fine, fitting all the little dresses just right, but I looked such a fool in the only one my size that Mum threw it back on the pile. (Naomi tried it on instead and looked gorgeous, but then she always does.) Funny-Face was delving in a sack of boys' clothes so I sifted through it too and found some jeans and a sweater and a really great baseball bomber jacket with a picture of a lion on the back!

"Well, we're all dressed up but we've still got no place to go," said Mack.

But he was wrong.

Oh, you'll never guess where we ended up!

Someone from Social Services and the man from the Housing Office came around to the church hall to tell us. We were all going to be temporarily accommodated in another hotel. Not a special bed-and-breakfast dumping ground. A *real* hotel. The Star Hotel. With stars after its name.

When we stepped through those starry glass
doors it was like finding fairyland. There were
soft sofas all over the reception area, and a thick
red carpet, and flowers in great vases, and a huge
chandelier sparkled from the ceiling. All of us
from the O yal Htl crowded into the reception
area, and Mum and Mack and Naomi's mum and

Funny-Face's mum and dad and all the other grownups sprawled on the sofas while we all ran round and round the red carpet and up and down the wide staircase and rang all the bells on the lifts.

The Star Manager came out of his office to meet us. He didn't look terribly thrilled to see us, but he shook us all by the hand, even the littlest stickiest kid, and welcomed us to the Star Hotel. Then there was a lot of talk and fuss about rooms, with the Manager and his chief receptionist going into a huddle. This receptionist was dark instead of blonde, and fierce instead of fluffy, but she also had long pointy fingernails and she started to tap them very impatiently indeed. But at last it was all sorted out and she handed all of us little cards instead of keys.

We were in suite 13. It might be an unlucky number for some people, but it was lucky lucky lucky for us.

Note I said suite, not room. As we shot up one floor in the lift and padded along the thickly carpeted corridor, Pippa licked her lips hopefully, thinking we were going to be given a sweety sweet. Even I didn't understand what suite really meant.

Suite 13 wasn't just one room. It was a set of

three rooms, just like a little apartment. Only there was nothing little about suite 13. It was really big—and *beautiful*. The main room was blue, with deeper blue velvet curtains and a dark blue coverlet on the huge bed. There was a painting on the wall of a boy in a blue velvet suit and a blue glass vase on the bedside table filled with little blue pretendy rosebuds. There was a dressing table with swivel mirrors so you could see the back of your head, and a blue leather folder containing notepaper and envelopes, and a blue felttip pen patterned with stars. There was a big television too—a color one—and it even had cable!

There was a bathroom leading off this main room. It was blue too, with a blue bath, blue sink,

even a blue loo. They all shone like the sea they were so sparkly clean. Laid out on the gleaming tiled shelf were little blue bottles of shampoo and bath gel and tiny cakes of forget-me-not soap. Mum sniffed them rapturously, her eyes shining.

Mack kicked his shoes off and lay on the big bed, Hank sitting astride his tummy. The bed was so big that even Mack could fit right inside it, and his feet wouldn't stick out at the end. I thought we might *all* have fit inside it, because it was the only bed in the room.

Then I saw another door and opened it. There was another bedroom, with three single beds, three little tables, and three little wooden chairs with carved hearts and painted roses. It was just like the three bears fairy story—and there were

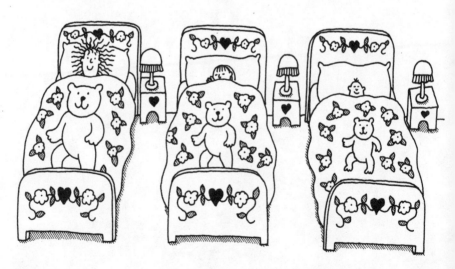

bears on the blankets too, and a painting of Goldilocks up on the wall. The carpet and wallpaper were pale blue but the ceiling was a deep navy, with stars scattered all over it. That night when I slept in my wonderful, soft, splendid Bed Number Nine I could still see the stars, even with the light switched off. They glowed luminously in the dark, my own magic midnight stars. I didn't want to sleep, just in case this was all a wonderful dream and when I woke up I'd be back in the grotty old Oyal Htl.

But it wasn't a dream at all. I woke up early and lay luxuriating in my bed and then I crept into mum and Mack's room. They were all cuddled up together, looking friendly even though they were fast asleep. I sat down at the dressing table and practiced a few funny faces and then I took a piece of paper and the felt-tip pen and wrote letters to all my friends.

*** Star Hotel ***

Dear Jamie,

I hope you haven't forgot me, I'm Elsa, and I don't like my new school much but I do like my new home. It's ever such a posh hotel and if it's nearer your school maybe I can come back which would be GREAT.

Love from Elsa

P.S. I'm the girl they said was thick but you said I was INTELLIGENT.

**★★★ Star Hotel ★★★**

Dear Mrs. Hoover, Sorry
Mrs. Macpherson,
     Hey, this hotel is
HEAPS better than the Royal.
Why don't you come and work
here? I bet you'd like it and
I'd give you a hand. The walls
have all got fancy paper so
no one ever scribbles on them.
                Love from Elsa

**★★★ Star Hotel ★★★**

Dear Naomi,
     Isn't it super here. My
bedroom's got stars on the
ceiling, has yours? I hope we
don't have to go back to the
Royal for ages and ages.
See you at breakfast.
     Love from your friend Elsa
                X X X

**★★★ Star Hotel ★★★**

Dear Funny-Face,
     There are lots of bushes
and trees and stuff at the
end of the Star Hotel garden
so maybe we could make
a camp ???
                See you.
                     Elsa

**★★★ Star Hotel ★★★**

Dear Pippa,
     I will read you this letter
seeing as you can't read
yet yourself. It is from me,
Elsa, and it's just to say
HELLO and we'll play lots
today.
     Love from your big sister
                     Elsa

XXXXXXXXXXXXX

Dear Hank,
Hello Big Baby

Love from your big
sister Elsa

X X X

Dear Mum,
It's so lovely here I don't
think you'll ever be sad
or cross ever again, eh?
Lots and lots of love
from Elsa

X X X X X X X X X X X X X

Dear Mack,
Och Aye the Noo.
That's all the Scotch
I know.
From Elsa

Dear Elsa,
I am having a lovely time
here. I have been writing
lots and lots of letters. I even
wrote one to the warthog !!!
But I am too happy to hate
anyone and there are stars
on my ceiling and I have
stars in my eyes because it
is so super here at the Star
Hotel. Love and X X X
From Elsa

203

There!  I used up all the notepaper and gave myself a big appetite for breakfast.

Ooooh the breakfast!  You have it in a lovely room with a dark pink swirly carpet and pink fuzzy paper on the walls and rose-pink cloths on the tables.  You sit at a table and spread a rose-pink napkin on your lap and a waitress in a black dress and a white apron comes and asks what you want to drink.  Then you go and help yourself to whatever you want to eat from the breakfast bar. You can have whatever you want.  Lots and lots and lots of it.

Even Mum had more breakfast than usual. She had freshly squeezed orange juice and black coffee and toast and butter and marmalade.

Mack had tea and a bowl of porridge because he's Scottish and then he had a big plate of bacon

and egg and mushroom and fried potatoes and more bacon because that's his favorite, and he tucked the extra bacon into toast to make a bacon sandwich.

Pippa didn't copy me! She chose all by herself. Apple juice and Cocoa Pops and milk and a soft white roll and butter and honey.

Hank had hot milk and a little bowl of porridge like his dad and a runny egg and tiny toast soldiers. He loved this breakfast and wanted to wave his arms about to show his appreciation and he dropped a few crumbs (more than a few, actually) on the carpet, but no one seemed to mind and the waitress tickled him under the chin and said he was a chubby little cherub!

Mum and Mack and Pippa and Hank all knew exactly what they wanted for breakfast. I was the one who simply couldn't decide because it all looked so delicious. So guess what. I had almost all of it.

I had milky tea and cranberry juice and corn-flakes sprinkled with rainbow sugar and then muesli with extra raisins and apple rings and then

scrambled egg on toast with tomato sauce and then sausages stuck in a long roll to make a hot dog and then a big jammy Danish pastry and I ate it all up, every little bit. It was the best breakfast ever.

What with the cranberry juice and the cherry jam in the pastry I ended up looking like Dracula. And that reminded me of a Dracula breakfast joke and that got me started.

I told jokes to Mum and Mack and Pippa and Hank and I shouted them to Naomi and Funny-Face across the tables and I tried them out on our waitress too because she seemed friendly and said I was amazing.

Do you want to hear a small sample?

What does Dracula like for breakfast?
*Dreaded wheat.*

What do mermaids eat for breakfast?
*Mermalade!*

What do cannibals like for breakfast?
*Buttered host.*

What do cats prefer for breakfast?
*Mice Krispies.*

How would a cannibal describe a man in a hammock?
*Breakfast in bed.*

What happens when a baby eats Rice Krispies?
*It goes snap, crackle and poop.*

I *must* stop rabbiting on like this. Well. Just one more.

What do you get if you pour boiling water down a rabbit hole?
*Hot cross bunnies!*

I'm not hot. I feel super-cool.
I'm not cross, I'm happy happy happy.
I'm not a bunny. I'm Elsa and I roar like a lion.

Hey, what do you get if you cross a lion with a parrot?
*I don't know, but if he says "Pretty Polly" you'd better*
*SMILE*